# THE

# WELLER

## Adam J. Whitlatch

*To Dave,*
*May you never know*
*thirst!*

*Best*

LATCHKEY
PRESS

THIRD EDITION

The Weller

Published by Latchkey Press

ISBN-13: 978-0615820125
ISBN-10: 0615820123

Original artwork *Desert Punk* Copyright 2011 Peter Allen / MisC:
http://miscee.deviantart.com

Font work and cover alteration Copyright 2013 K.H. Koehler

# Also by Adam J. Whitlatch

*Birthright – Book I of the Temujin Saga*

*War of the Worlds: Goliath*

*In loving memory of my grandfather, Gene Freeborn, who loved to end a long day on the farm in his favorite chair with a good western novel. This one's for you, Grandpa.*

# Acknowledgments

This book wouldn't have been possible without the love and support of my beautiful wife, Jessica, who put up with my late hours and dragging my iPad to family functions to work instead of socializing.

Special thanks to my parents, Al and Jan Whitlatch, for helping me keep the lights on while I wrote the book. Dad, thank you for insisting that I "write more of those *Weller* stories." Mom, thank you for patiently reading draft after draft.

Thanks to my big brother and mechanic, Perry, for sharing his knowledge with me.

My eternal gratitude to Shannon Ryan for mercilessly picking apart the first draft. One couldn't ask for a better beta reader.

Thank you to my good friend, Patrick Koozy, for allowing me to use his name and likeness in the book. You're a good guy, Patrick. I don't care what those wasteland peasants say about you.

And of course, thank you to the KHP crew, S.D. Hintz, Jerrod Balzer, K.H. Koehler, and Louise Bohmer, for having faith in *The Weller* and also in me.

# Introduction

Never in our wildest dreams did we imagine it could happen to us. We, the mighty, felt confident in our national security. The idea that the United States could possibly lose a nuclear war was considered not only unlikely, but pure fantasy. When the bombs fell on that cold October morning, fantasy became reality. Our enemies, having grown tired of our endless meddling in the affairs of tiny third-world nations, carved their maxim into our collective spirit with the ink of nuclear fire, "Yankees, go home!"

Of course we returned fire, and we fought valiantly... for about eleven and a half minutes. That's how long it took from the moment the first bombs fell on Washington, D.C. until the last blast wiped San Francisco off the map. Although the war was swift, our suffering was not. The combined impact of nuclear, chemical, and biological weapons rendered the human race essentially crippled.

The electromagnetic pulse generated by the nuclear weapons wiped out our advanced technology, effectively driving humanity back to the age of steam engines. Vehicles manufactured during the computer era that were indirectly affected by EMP quickly fell into disrepair as the means to maintain them were no longer readily available. Powerful, previously unheard of plagues wiped out entire metropolitan areas in a matter of days - the fruits of our scientific labors in the name of preserving the American way of life. But all of these tragedies paled in comparison to the most crushing casualty of the Twelve Minute War.

*Water.*

An estimated seventy percent of the Earth's drinkable water was rendered unfit for consumption, the result of the combined cataclysmic effects of nuclear, chemical, and biological agents. People panicked as they began to gather and hoard any and all sources of pure water for their own personal use, foolishly gorging themselves and squandering their supplies until they realized their error. Water soon became the new world currency, outweighing even gold on the bargaining table. Entire communities were forced to drink water that, before the war, would have been considered unsuitable for livestock. The cleanest water was saved for use in trade.

In the major cities, the controversial practice of "distilling" was quickly brought into use to curb the growing water shortage. As any schoolboy knows, the human body is roughly sixty-five percent water; the actual percentage varies depending on body mass and age. Facilities intended for the harvesting and bottling of this water from the bodies of the dead sprang up virtually overnight. Traditional funerals and cremation became outlawed in these areas, and the penalty for violation was death - immediately followed by distillation. Some facilities, however, did not wait for the donors to die, instead harvesting the water from those unable to fight back, kidnapping unwilling donors from small villages deep in the wastelands.

Outside the cities, where people still put morals before their thirst, small towns would contract men to search for potable water, trading for food, lodging, fuel, and even female companionship. These people became colloquially known throughout the wastelands as "wellers" due to the practice of seeking out and raiding forgotten wells and occasionally digging new ones where abundant sources of uncontaminated ground water could be found. Wellers quickly became the targets of roadside bandits and pirates, and thus began taking extreme measures to protect themselves and their cargo. Soon, the once noble wellers were reduced to mere mercenaries and pirates themselves, seeking out the cleanest water for those willing to pay handsomely for it.

However, not all wellers chose to become puppets of the rich man...

Some became legends.

*"It is wise to bring some water, when one goes out to look for water."*
- Arab Proverb

*"There is enough water for human need, but not for human greed."*
- Mahatma Gandhi

*"When the well is dry, we learn the worth of water."*
- Benjamin Franklin

# PART I
# ROAD RUNNER

# One

The weller closed his eyes and sighed contentedly as the whore rolled off of him. Her chest heaved with exhaustion as she hooked one long leg over his and laid her head on his shoulder. Her breath was hot and raspy in his ear; it smelled like moonshine and decay.

"Oh, *God*, baby," she gasped, running her fingers through his untidy mess of red hair. "That was *incredible*."

"Uh huh," he said.

"No, I mean it," she insisted. "I haven't been fucked like that since..." She sighed.

The weller grunted. His money was on "yesterday."

He looked around the dilapidated motel room. Dust, stirred up by their lovemaking, floated in the air illuminated by the fading sunlight filtering though the tattered, rodent-gnawed curtains. It would be dark soon. In the fading light, he could see a cheap print of a woman in a blue dress surrounded by wild flowers hanging on the wall; somebody had drawn lopsided nipples on the woman's breasts with a black marker.

He sat up and looked down at the woman he shared a bed with; she writhed on the stained comforter and smiled. She'd been pretty once, he could tell, but now she was another desert burnout. Three of her teeth were missing, and the others looked to soon be joining them. Her sun-bleached hair clung to her breasts, damp with sweat. Life in the wastes had done this woman no favors.

Still, she was the cleanest-looking whore he'd come across since leaving Colorado. And after two months of scouring the seemingly endless flat Nebraska wastes, a man needed something with a few curves to look at. And this whore certainly had those. He sighed and rubbed his eyes, his finger lingering on the thick white scar cutting across his forehead down to the bridge of his nose.

Without a word, he retrieved his blue jeans from the tangled heap on the floor beside the bed and stood to pull them on.

"Where are you going?"

The weller bent to pick up his boots. "It'll be dark soon. Best to be moving on."

The whore pouted. "Come on back to bed. I still have a few tricks to show you."

"You've earned your pay."

The whore looked over at the one-quart pickle jar full of water on the nightstand. She licked her dry, cracked lips as she looked at the crystal clear liquid inside.

"Now get dressed," said the weller as he knelt to tie his boots. "And go."

"Are you sure you don't want to keep me for just a little bit longer?" she asked.

"Get out."

"Your loss."

The weller shrugged. "I'll live."

*Click.*

The weller squeezed his eyes shut. *Damn.* Slowly, he turned and looked at the whore, who was kneeling on the bed with a .38 pointed at his head.

"I wouldn't be so sure 'bout that," she said, all sweetness gone from her voice.

The weller pointed at the .38. "Now just where were you hiding *that?*"

She smiled.

He smirked. "That *is* a neat trick."

3

"Shut up," she snapped. "Give me your keys."

The weller glanced down at the chair to his left. Resting there on the stained upholstery was a mammoth revolver - .50 caliber, with two upper and lower barrels and a heavy wooden grip. Inscribed down the length of the gap between the barrels were the words "THE WELL DIGGER" in large block letters. The chair was a good two steps away; he'd be dead before he reached it.

"I got 'im, Hank!" the whore shouted with a triumphant grin.

The weller heard a muffled *whoop* through the door, followed by the faint sound of rapidly retreating footfalls. The bitch's goddamned pimp had been listening, waiting for him to let down his guard. He turned his eyes back to the whore, and she smiled as she slithered off the bed, careful to keep her gun trained on him.

"I wasn't kidding, you know," she said. "You really are a *great* fuck."

The weller snorted. "I've had better."

"Fuck you!"

"Once was enough."

"Come on, baby!" Hank called from outside.

The whore held out her hand. "Keys. Now."

The weller hesitated, trying to think of any possible way out of this with his skin intact. A blood-curdling scream rang out from the parking lot, and the whore whirled toward the door, taking her eyes off her prisoner.

"Hank?" she shrieked.

The weller dove for the chair and grabbed the Well Digger. He rolled onto his side and took a wild shot at the whore. The gun's report was as loud as the voice of God and rumbled off the paper-thin walls. The massive bullet tore through the whore's chest and exploded out her back, showering the wall and bedspread with blood.

The .38 in her hand went off, but the shot hit the ceiling and peppered the weller's hair with plaster dust. He lay there a moment, waiting for the ringing in his ears to subside. Slowly he got to his feet and stared down at the whore's ruined corpse lying on the bed. He looked at the gaping hole in her chest where her heart used to be, at the bloody and smoking remains of her left breast, and sighed.

"What a waste," he said as he flipped open the breech and plucked out the spent shell casing. "Perfectly good bullet."

He slammed a fresh cartridge into the smoking hole and snapped the breech shut. He placed the Well Digger on the bed and resumed dressing. There was no need to hurry. He knew exactly where Hank would be.

*****

The weller emerged from the motel room fully dressed in tattered blue jeans, a black t-shirt, and a sun-faded brown oilskin duster. A faded red and white bandana was tied loosely around his neck, and amber-tinted ski goggles rode high on his forehead. His boots, black, heavy and steel-plated at the toes and heels, thumped on the warped and broken boardwalk. In his left hand, he held the Well Digger, and the jar of water in the other. The dead whore wouldn't need it where she was going. The ferryman only dealt in cold hard cash.

It didn't take long to find the pimp; the smell of burning flesh led the way. The weller stepped off the sun-bleached planks toward the only two vehicles in the parking lot: a primer-gray mid-seventies Buick Regal and red Jeep Wrangler; it was the latter of these two that he approached. When he rounded the Jeep and came to the driver's side, he saw the pimp, Hank, sitting unconscious on the ground by the door. His hand was fused to the handle; wisps of smoke rose from the melted mass of metal and flesh.

The weller shook his head and clicked his tongue as he holstered his gun beneath his coat. He placed the water jar on the ground near the pimp and walked to the rear of the Jeep. He lay down on his back and slid beneath the vehicle. There, in the Jeep's shadow, was a wooden box partitioned off into four sections, each containing a car battery. Jumper cables connected to two of the batteries snaked off to two metal posts protruding from the frame. The weller disconnected the leads and slid out from underneath.

He lifted a tarp in the back of the Jeep and traded the box of batteries for a crowbar. He hefted the tool as he walked back to where Hank still lay comatose. He studied the pimp for a moment, and then shoved the flat end of the crowbar between Hank's hand and the melted metal of the door handle. He jerked the bar, and the pimp roared back to consciousness as his hand was ripped away from the door, leaving ragged, bloody flesh behind.

The pimp screamed and clutched his ruined hand to his chest, but the weller ignored him. He used the crowbar to break the grisly mound of metal and cooked meat from the door, and then quickly scooped up the jar on the ground before Hank's kicking feet could damage it. He placed the jar, along with the bloody crowbar, inside the Jeep.

"You p-piece of shit," Hank spat. "I'll kill you!"

"Yeah, we saw how well that worked out for you the last time, didn't we?" said the weller lazily as he reached into the Jeep to open the door from the inside.

The roar of the engine drowned the pimp's curses out as the weller turned the key. As he put the Jeep in reverse, he saw Hank sitting up with a .45 in his hand. The weller stepped on the gas and threw open the door. Hank barely had time to scream before the door connected with his face and slammed him back down into the dirt.

The weller never looked back. He steered the Jeep toward the two-lane and turned east, leaving Hank bleeding in the dirt with one good hand and a dead whore.

# Two

Matt Freeborn stared with bleary eyes through the dust-coated windshield as the Jeep rocketed across the darkened wastes. Concentrating on the road wasn't the hard part; it was staving off the never-ending boredom from looking at it for so long. Nebraska had to be the flattest, most featureless stretch of wasteland Matt ever had the misfortune of driving into, but he had gone too far to turn back now. It was either press on or turn around and see the same scenery all over again from a whole new angle.

Fuck that.

The only sounds were the roar of the ancient engine and the constant impacts of the weeds that grew out of the cracked asphalt striking the Jeep's bumper. The desolate two-lane highway offered few obstacles and even fewer distractions. It had been hours since Matt had seen any rusted out husks of vehicles abandoned after the war. No debris. Just the endless, flat road and the sound of the Jeep passing over it.

Matt reached over to the passenger seat and picked up the glass jar meant to be payment for the evening's romp. He took his hand off the wheel briefly to break the wax seal. Carefully, so as not to spill a single drop, he took a drink. Not a long one; he never took long drinks. It was the key to surviving out in the wastes.

The water was clean, with no distracting flavors or odor. It was good. Too good to waste on some mangy desert whore and her

7

double-crossing pimp, no matter how talented her tongue had been. But, unfortunately, that was the way of things out in the wastes. The best things in life were not, as it turned out, free. They cost water, and the cleaner the better.

Matt knew the price of such luxury well. His body bore the scars of all the times when he'd paid for his water dearly with his body's own moisture. Blood, sweat, and tears; it hardly seemed a fair trade after almost ten years of it, but at least he still had his skin, which was more than he could say for most of the other wellers he had known.

In terms of risk, welling ranked somewhere between snake hunting and law keeping. Having a bag full of rattling water jars was like having a target painted on your chest, and every time Matt strolled into a town to peddle his wares he was gambling with his life. Hardly a day went by when some rat bastard didn't make an attempt on his bag or his hide, but then they'd meet the Well Digger.

He took another sip and replaced the lid. He shook his head and blinked his bloodshot eyes. Up ahead, the sky above the horizon began to take on an orange hue. Soon he would have to find shelter from the desert sun, and that meant welling.

He reached over to open the glove box and pulled out a back-folded Nebraska road map, taking his eyes off the road to find his position. He squinted as the rising sun cast a harsh glare through the windshield and raised the map to shield his eyes. There were a few options within a twenty-mile radius, some that looked more promising than others, and even a few that looked like they could potentially still be inhabited. That never worked for welling; some native would always try to claim ownership of the weller's prize, and that was trouble better avoided.

Matt had decided on a small town on a northern side road when a loud bang reverberated inside the Jeep, and the entire vehicle shuddered, punctuated by a metallic scraping sound. He batted the map aside and took the wheel in both hands, fighting to keep the Jeep under control as he stomped the brake pedal to the floor and bright orange sparks flew up from the pavement. When the Jeep finally came to a complete stop, he looked through the windshield across the hood. There, imbedded in the front of his Jeep, was a heap of rusty, twisted metal.

"Shit!" He punched the steering wheel.

*****

Matt cursed and kicked a tire as he passed, his eyes locked on the white cloud of steam billowing through the twisted scrap in the Jeep's grill. He knelt down, studying the growing puddle of green coolant dripping from the radiator. The sand sucked up the fluid greedily, the first moisture it had probably seen in months.

"Lizard shit!" the weller spat.

He got to his feet and patted the dust from his jeans. He examined the metal for a moment and looped his fingers through the squared sections. With a strong tug, it pulled free with a grinding screech, and coolant poured even faster from the hole in the radiator. Matt held up the twisted hulk; he'd seen these before. Four wheels, a deep basket of metal mesh, and a handle. They were usually found inside stores, but it wasn't uncommon to find them littering the streets in urban areas.

This one still contained the decaying remnants of colored cloth, as well as empty tin cans. Nomads often used these carts to transport their belongings across long distances on foot. Obviously the owner of this cart never reached their intended destination. He tossed the debris aside with a grunt and returned to the Jeep.

He reached out to lift the hood, but pulled back quickly, his hands burned by the scalding steam issuing from underneath. He hissed in pain and placed his fingers to his lips, sucking on the blisters already rising on his skin.

"Mother fu—" he growled around his fingertips. "Ow!"

He took a step back and thought for a moment, trying to decide his next course of action. He turned, shaded his eyes from the early-morning sun and looked east toward the next town. Waves of heat distorted his vision, but he could see the vague outline of a small city on the horizon. He retrieved the map from the passenger seat and checked his location.

"Holdrege," he muttered.

9

Normally he preferred to stay away from larger settlements, sticking instead to the small wasteland villages where he might be able to do respectable business. Cities - no matter how small - as a rule were generally unfriendly to wellers; too many street gangs and corporate water-seekers to contend with. No, Matt preferred low profile, but his vehicle needed tending to.

He needed a mechanic. And he needed one *now*.

According to the map, Holdrege, Nebraska had been a city of over five thousand souls before the war. Certainly that number had been more than quartered in the subsequent years, but chances of a town that size still having a half-decent grease monkey were as good as anyone could hope for. Matt ran his blistered fingers through his untidy mop of bright red hair and sighed. He glanced across the wastes at the distant city and back to his steaming Jeep, then back to the city again.

High above him, a flock of turkey vultures were beginning to circle. The silent scavengers soared, wings eerily still as they glided on the hot desert winds. That was enough for Matt.

Holdrege it was, then. He turned and walked toward the rear of the Jeep.

He lifted the tarp and tossed it aside, uncovering several plastic and glass containers of various sizes. Most of them contained water, and others contained gasoline or oil. Matt reached into the Jeep and lifted out a one-gallon milk jug marked "BAD" in red permanent marker. A few ounces of brown water slid around the bottom of the jug. He tossed it aside and reached for another, similarly labeled, but found it only a quarter full.

"Great," he muttered.

He kept these jugs around for situations like this, but had neglected a refill the last time he used them; gathering contaminated water wasn't usually in his job description. He sighed and sloshed the rainbow-tinged water in the jug before combining the few ounces of brown liquid. He walked back to the front of the Jeep and looked down at the stream of fluid pouring from the radiator, now not so much of an arc as a dribble. He emptied the jug into the radiator's gaping mouth, but it wasn't enough. He tossed it aside and stepped up onto the bumper, balancing as he fumbled with his fly.

He looked down at the radiator, adjusted his aim, and waited for the stream.

And waited.

Waited.

He looked down. "Oh, c'mon! Don't get bashful on me now!"

He hopped up and down and closed his eyes, envisioning glistening wells and bubbling streams, but when he opened his eyes, the only stream was the one issuing out of the radiator onto his boots.

"Shit!"

He hopped down and returned to the back of the Jeep. He picked up another jug filled nearly to the top with crystal clear water. He reflexively licked his lips at the sight and sound of the sloshing liquid. It broke his heart knowing what he was about to do with it.

Some folks called wellers scavengers and bandits. Others called them heroes. A scant few considered them to be the only *true* law left in the wastelands. To Matt Freeborn it was an honest living, one he worked very hard at. That's why the thought of pouring enough water to buy him either two good horses or a wife with a full set of white teeth down into a leaking radiator absolutely killed him inside.

*****

The mechanic peeked out from under the hood at Matt and - showing a mouthful of broken, blackened teeth - said, "Radiator's got a hole in it!"

Matt slumped back in the driver's seat and feigned shock. *"No shit?"*

"No shit!" said the grease monkey jovially, obviously unaccustomed to sarcasm.

"You know..." Matt slapped the steering wheel with his palm. "That *might* just account for that long wet trail that followed me *all the way* into town!"

"Sure'n it might!" the grease monkey agreed.

11

Matt smacked his forehead on the steering wheel in frustration, honking the horn twice. Without looking up at the simple-minded mechanic, he asked, "How long?"

The mechanic shrugged. "Not too long. Want me to check the hoses and the oil?"

"Sure," said Matt, stepping out of the Jeep. "Hell, as long as I'm getting fucked, might as well be thorough. No sense in going all half-assed about it."

The grease monkey grinned. "I like you, mister."

"Yeah." Matt chose the chair along the shop wall with the fewest stains on it and sat down. "I'll bet you do, pal."

He picked through the various wrinkled magazines that littered the tilting table beside him. There were several nudie books, but when he tried to flip though the first one and failed on account of the pages being stuck together, he tossed it aside in disgust and wiped his hands on his jeans.

Finally, he chose a badly sun-faded copy of the *Weekly World News*. He read that, before the war, strange little gray men had come from the stars to kidnap people and a grotesque bat-like child with razor-sharp teeth terrorized the nation by biting several children, but had later gone on record to offer his endorsement to the Democratic presidential candidate... whatever the hell *that* was. Matt was shocked; he could hardly believe his eyes, yet this was, after all, the news. That meant it *had* to be true.

Cramped in the narrow chair, Matt reached into his coat and pulled the Well Digger from the holster on his left hip and placed it on top of the magazines beside him.

The mechanic looked up from his work and stared across the shop at the massive weapon for a moment. He hesitated briefly, licking his lips, and called out, "Hey, how much you want fer that there fancy shooter?"

"Your soul," said Matt, not glancing up from his magazine. "Get back to work, grease monkey."

The mechanic nodded and returned to his work without another word. For a few more minutes, Matt was able to read uninterrupted, mesmerized by the tale of how American soldiers captured Satan in a far away land called Iraq. Suddenly, he felt an annoying tickle in his nose. It persisted until he sneezed, spraying dusty snot all over the supermarket tabloid.

He looked up and saw the mechanic carefully pouring black powder into the open radiator from a small glass cylinder. Some of it floated on the warm breeze blowing through the shop. For a moment, Matt pondered the powder, some of which was still lodged deep in his nostrils. Suddenly it dawned on him...

The glass cylinder was a pepper shaker.

Matt leaped to his feet and scooped up the Well Digger in one fluid motion. Enraged, he stalked over to the mechanic, placed the gun against the man's head and cocked back the hammer.

"What do you think you're doing to my Jeep?"

Tobacco juice dribbled from the startled mechanic's chin as he held up the shaker. "I-it's only p-p-pepper!"

"I can see it's pepper," Matt growled, pressing the twin barrels harder against the grease monkey's skull. "What in blue blazes are you doing pouring it into *my* radiator?"

"I'm fixing it!"

"Are you touched in the head? How in God's name is *pepper* supposed to fix the hole in my radiator?"

"I-it plugs up the hole," the mechanic wailed, his words slurring together as he sobbed. "It flows through until it finds the hole. And then it plugs it up and hardens and stops the leak."

Matt cocked his head, bewildered by the mechanic's statement. "No shit?"

"No shit. I swear."

"You can really do that with just regular old table pepper?" Matt relaxed his hold with the Well Digger slightly. "Seriously? As simple as that?"

"Yes'ir! Just plain ol' table pepper. Simple as that, yes'ir."

"Well, I'll be damned." Matt dropped the Well Digger into its holster. "Sorry, I, uh—"

The mechanic nodded, his eyes fixed intently on the grease-stained floor.

"So." Matt cleared his throat. "Is that it?"

"Yup!" said the mechanic, retrieving a grime-covered yellow jug of engine coolant from a nearby shelf. "Hoses look good. Air filter just needed a quick shake out. Oil doesn't look too bad. Just let me top 'er off here. Then we'll start 'er up, and you'll be on your way."

As the mechanic screwed the cap back onto the radiator, Matt leaned into the cab and twisted the key in the ignition. The engine turned sluggishly for a moment before finally turning over and roaring to life. Matt rejoined the mechanic, and together they watched as the trickle of green fluid coming from the front center of the radiator slowed and, finally, stopped.

"I'll be damned." Matt looked up at the mechanic with an amazed grin. "Pepper!"

The grease monkey smiled and nodded. "Pepper."

Matt walked to the rear of the Jeep. "How much do I owe ya?"

"Well, let's see..." The mechanic adjusted his grease-stained cap on his balding head. "That all depends on what you've got. I trade for food, liquor, fuel, and—"

Matt returned to the front of the Jeep with a large canvas satchel. He reached into the bag, pulled out a Mason jar filled to the top with crystal clear water, and set it down on the hood.

"Water," said the mechanic, his voice distant.

"That enough?"

"Uh..." The mechanic licked his lips greedily. "Well, now, there's the coolant I added, and the pepper. That stuff's not cheap, y'know. And then of course there's the labor."

Matt pulled a second jar from the bag and placed it beside the first. The mechanic looked into his eyes and saw precious little generosity, and even less patience.

"Yes'ir." The mechanic nodded. "That oughtta just about cover it."

"Good," said Matt. "I'll get out of your hair then and be on my merry way."

*****

Two blocks away, a pair of dark eyes squinted through camouflage binoculars. The hands holding the spyglasses twisted, focusing the lenses on the outlander in the mechanic's shop. More importantly, they focused on the two gleaming jars sitting on the hood of the Jeep. The man lowered the binoculars and licked his chapped lips while he thoughtfully stroked his mustache. This wasn't just any outlander.

This was a weller.

"Powder," said the man.

From behind him stepped a short, rail-thin boy in his late teens. The boy's nostrils were red and raw, unsurprising from the way he kept rubbing his nose furiously.

"Yeah, boss?" the youth said.

"Go round up the boys." The man raised the binoculars for a second look.

He watched as the Jeep backed out of the garage slowly and then tore down the street, heading straight for US-34.

"We're going hunting."

# **Three**

Matt suppressed a yawn as his fingers twisted on the steering wheel. He'd been driving all night even before the radiator had eaten up most of his day. He knew he'd have to get off the road soon, but he wanted to put as many miles between himself and Holdrege as humanly possible before he did.

For a moment, he caught a glimpse of something shimmering in his rearview mirror. He blinked and looked again, but it was gone. Convinced it was his sleep-deprived mind playing tricks on him, he settled back in his seat.

Then he saw it again.

This time he knew his mind wasn't playing tricks on him, because the glint on the horizon was followed by another, and another, and another, until his mirror was filled with the shimmer of sunlight on windshields. This, he knew, could only mean one thing.

"Shit," he cursed, eyeing the mirror. "Road pirates."

He dropped the Jeep into fifth gear, and the ancient vehicle surged ahead with a reluctant roar. A glance at the mirror told him he was screwed; he counted nearly a dozen pirate vehicles gaining on him fast. There was no way the decrepit Jeep could outrun them, and he was fairly certain he couldn't fight them all off.

He reached into his coat for the Well Digger and disengaged the lower safety, switching the weapon to double-barreled firing. He placed the gun on the passenger seat within easy reach, gritted his teeth, and punched the wheel.

"Fuck!"

As the needle on the speedometer passed one hundred miles-per-hour, Matt glanced in the mirror. The lead car was now close enough that he could tell what color it was. The light blue Crown Victoria was coming up fast. This wasn't the first car of its kind Matt had ever seen. His grandfather had always referred to them as "squad cars."

He studied the lead vehicle with quick glances into the mirror. It had broken domes of red and blue glass on the roof. Despite the damage to the body, Matt could tell the car had curves, more than most vehicles on the road these days. He struggled to remember what his grandfather had told him about curvy cars.

They had *com pyewters.*

That was it. Curvy cars like the one leading the charge had *com pyewters.* And *lektroniks.* Matt didn't know what those were, but he knew what it meant.

It meant they broke *very* easily.

After the war, the newest cars with the *com pyewters* and *lektroniks* were the first to go. They were simply too hard to maintain; too many complex components meant too many things could go wrong. That meant Matt had an advantage over the leader of the pirates. He had the better vehicle.

In theory.

One of the vehicles, a small hatchback, broke free from the formation and sped up alongside the Jeep. A scout. Matt lifted the Well Digger, keeping it close to his chest as the vehicle drew up closer. The driver had a long, gaunt face with giant goggles that made him look like some demented insect; these protected him from the wind roaring through the broken windshield.

The pirate stuck out his tongue and cackled, an action that might have intimidated some nomads, but only made Matt smirk. The first blow of what was sure to be a grueling battle was struck when the weller calmly stuck his gun hand out the window and fired into the vehicle. The Well Digger's report echoed across the plain and

17

the pirate's head exploded, painting the interior of the car a dark crimson. The headless corpse slumped against the wheel and the hatchback drifted across the centerline, crashing into the side of the Jeep.

Matt fought with the wheel and forced the hatchback across the road, sending it careening into the ditch. He allowed himself a grunt of triumph, but knew the worst was yet to come. Angered by his preemptive strike, the pirates surged ahead in force. Two vehicles, a truck and a Ford sedan, flanked him while a van boxed him in from behind. Sure that they had him trapped, the passenger of the truck raised a crossbow.

Matt waited for the pirate to take aim and slammed down hard on the brakes. They squealed and were punctuated by the crunching of metal and plastic as the van crashed into the back of the Jeep. Matt watched as the crossbow bolt flew through the air in front of him, trailing a line behind it. It plunged through the cheek of the sedan's driver, who wrenched his wheel to the right in shock. The action simultaneously pulled the injured driver against his door and jerked the crossbow-wielding pirate through the window.

The Jeep's wheels crushed the pirate's legs and the vehicle bounced. Matt smirked, but then the van rammed into the Jeep a second time, chipping away even further at the back of the damaged vehicle. Matt was thrown forward in his seat, and his chest slammed into the steering wheel. He cursed as another impact knocked the Well Digger from his grip, and it fell to the floorboard below his feet.

As he felt blindly under the seat, a shot rang out and broken glass rained down on his head. He sat back up and found himself staring through a large hole in his windshield. A glance in the rearview mirror revealed a pirate sticking up from the van's sunroof; the man was reloading a double-barreled shotgun.

Furious, Matt threw open his door and, scooping up the Well Digger, grabbed the Jeep's roll bar with his left hand. He swung outward, clinging to the bar, and leveled the massive weapon at the front of the van. He squeezed the trigger, unloading both barrels into the van's radiator. Steam billowed and sparks flew from under the hood as oil and antifreeze sprayed up onto the windshield, blinding the driver and sending the vehicle into an erratic swerve. Matt smirked and reentered the Jeep.

The pirate wielding the shotgun was not yet incapacitated, however, and fired again. The van's wild swerving made the shot go wide, taking the Jeep's driver's side mirror off. Matt stomped on the brakes and let the van collide with the Jeep again. The impact took the wind out of the pirate's lungs, and the shotgun flew from his hands, clattering against the Jeep's roll bar before tumbling to the asphalt. Matt accelerated, leaving the crippled van lost in its own cloud of smoke.

The Crown Vic surged through the smoke and tore past the Jeep. The windows were dark, so Matt had no idea how many pirates might be inside. The Crown Vic whipped in front of him, cutting him off. He engaged the Well Digger's lower safety and fired a single round at the driver's side rear window. The car whipped to the left before the bullet broke through and exploded into the windshield a mere foot from the driver's head. Matt could now see inside the vehicle; the driver was alone.

He raised his gun again, but with only one shot left, he didn't dare risk wasting it. The Crown Vic was too agile. His best chance would be to force the car off the road. He squared the front of the Jeep up with the rear right corner of the pirate car. He then shifted back into fifth and used the Jeep's bumper as a battering ram. The jarring impact made the Crown Vic fishtail.

But that wasn't all.

Steam hissed from under the Jeep's hood, and green fluid splashed against the windshield. Sweet, poisonous antifreeze rained through the broken glass and coated Matt's face. He quickly pulled the ski goggles down over his eyes and tugged the bandana up over his nose.

The patch hadn't held!

"Fucking grease monkey!" he shouted, his curses muffled by the bandana.

The antifreeze coated the goggles, and he tried to clear them with his finger, but only succeeded in smearing them. He looked at the mirror and saw more pirates gaining on him fast. Knowing this might be his last chance to get away, he shoved the Well Digger through the hole in the windshield and took aim at the Crown Vic's broken window. He squinted, prayed for a clear shot, and squeezed the trigger.

The Well Digger roared, and through his smeared goggles, Matt could see a splash of red inside the car as the driver's body jerked. He'd winged the driver's right shoulder. The Crown Vic swerved and lost speed, allowing the smoking Jeep to pass.

The shower of antifreeze slowed and Matt removed his goggles. Through the smoke, he could see a bridge off in the distance. He remembered seeing a river on the map. Surely it was a dry bed, but maybe - just maybe - it would be deep enough to slow the pirates down.

Matt opened the glove box and pulled out a hand grenade. He'd come across the explosive many years ago inside an abandoned humvee and had been saving it for a special occasion. He checked the mirror and his distance to the rapidly approaching bridge. With no other options, he threw open the door and kissed the grenade. He waited until he was halfway across the bridge before he pulled the pin and dropped it.

He watched the tiny explosive bounce and roll on the crumbling concrete as a pirate car - this one little more than a frame and an engine - drove onto the bridge. He counted slowly; with every passing second, he feared the ancient weapon was a dud. Then the pirate car passed over it, and the air behind him erupted in a fireball, sending concrete shards and shrapnel in all directions.

Matt watched as a large section of the bridge, neglected for more than forty years and weakened by the combined explosions of the grenade and pirate car, crumbled and fell into the dry creek bed below. The chasm was deep enough that the pirates could not cross it in their vehicles. They would have to find another way around. In the mirror, the Crown Vic stopped short of the bridge. Matt smiled as the driver got out and shook his one good arm at the retreating Jeep.

His smile faded, however, as a red light on the instrument panel lit up beneath the coating of dust and fresh coolant. The Jeep was overheating, and all the pepper in the world wasn't going to save it this time. He would have to find a replacement, and soon. But first he needed to get off the road before the pirates found another way to get their vehicle across the riverbed.

A leaning and faded sign on the roadside offered salvation:
MINDEN, NEBRASKA
HOME OF HISTORIC 'FORT FRONTIER'
5 MILES

# Four

The engine block cracked outside of Minden. The rattling of the crippled engine echoed off the abandoned buildings lining the sand-strewn street. Matt scanned the decaying structures, looking for any suitable place to hide the Jeep. Soon it would be dark, and his headlights might attract unwanted attention - if the vehicle lasted that long.

He looked up and saw a sign, not unlike the other gimmicky tourist trap advertisements he'd seen along the road over the years. A rotting replica of a covered wagon sat atop a low-standing building, and on it were the words:

WELCOME TO FORT FRONTIER

Matt saw a complex of buildings surrounded by a high log wall. From the parking lot, he could see the visitors' entrance and a derelict motel, but nowhere to stow the Jeep. He kept driving until he came to a break in the wall; a rusted chain-link gate barred entry. Beyond it, he could see tall, semi-cylindrical metal buildings with large sliding doors.

Perfect.

Matt brought the clanking Jeep to a halt and got out. He reached into the back and pulled out a pair of bolt cutters. He worked them in his hands as he approached the gate. The heavily corroded chain snapped easily, and he pulled the gate aside with a grating squeak that echoed throughout the ghost town.

He looked over his shoulder, ensuring he was not being observed, and returned to the Jeep. The engine roared and clunked in protest, but, with enough coaxing, finally crossed the threshold into Fort Frontier. Matt drove toward the nearest building, but before he could reach it, the engine seized and died. A puddle of smoking oil pooled and expanded underneath the Jeep.

Matt sighed, both sickened by his dilemma and relieved by his progress. He retrieved the bolt cutters and got out. The padlock on the building was a heavy one, and - despite the corrosion - took two snaps from the cutters to break. The door, stationary for over forty years, resisted, and it took Matt nearly five minutes of pushing to open it wide enough to accept the Jeep.

He looked inside, but the sun had already set behind him and the building was pitch-black. He returned to the Jeep and flipped on the headlights, illuminating the interior. What he saw when he passed through the door was beyond his wildest dreams. If Matt Freeborn ever believed in God, it was at that moment.

The walls were lined with *cars*.

Matt whistled as his eyes roamed over the vehicles, all shapes and colors. Waist-high partitions of Plexiglas and steel piping formed protective barriers from long-dead tourists. He walked up to one of the cars - a dark green antique - and leaned over the partition to run his finger over the headlight bezel. His fingertip left a trail in the thick coating of dust and the chrome beneath glistened in the light. He looked down and saw a plaque mounted to the barrier. He knelt in front of it and blew away the layer of dust.

"1951 Chrysler Windsor," he read slowly.

The car was long, and had more curves than any vehicle he had ever seen before. He took three steps to his left and looked down at the next car, this one two different shades of blue.

He read the plaque aloud, "1955 Dodge Coronet."

He continued on like this until the distant illumination of the headlights failed him and he found it too dark to make out the vehicles' features, let alone read the plaques. At the end of the building was a gate. Beyond it, Matt could barely make out the upward slope of a ramp, easily wide enough for a car to travel on. He decided to store that bit of information away for later.

A loud bang startled him. He whirled and went down on one knee, the Well Digger trained on the open door. He watched as a gust of hot wind caught the door and pulled it slightly, and then let it fall back against the building. The door thundered, and the walls reverberated from the impact. Matt exhaled, suddenly aware that he'd been holding his breath.

He holstered the Well Digger and stood. There would be time for exploration later. First he had to finish what he came for.

*****

It hadn't taken long to push the Jeep inside and force the door shut once more, but the job had taken its toll on Matt's already aching body. He dug in the back of the Jeep until he found a rusted kerosene lantern. He held it up to his ear and shook it. The fuel inside sloshed loudly.

Good.

He struck a match and lit the wick, bathing the area in a soft glow. He walked over to the nearest car, this one a red Chrysler. Careful not to drop the lantern, he climbed over the partition separating him from his treasure. He knelt and touched the front passenger side tire.

The rubber had deteriorated some over the years since the war, but not as badly as if it had been exposed to the elements. There was no air pressure, but the tires still held their shape. This perplexed Matt until he brought the lamp down to the floor and looked underneath the car. The frame was held up by four steel jacks, which kept the weight off the tires and allowed them to keep the appearance of being inflated.

This place kept getting better and better. Pristine cars. Good tires. But would luck continue to hold?

Matt slithered underneath the car and rapped on the gas tank. A loud, hollow echo reached his ears, and he breathed a sigh of relief. This saved him the laborious task of draining useless pre-war sludge from the tanks. He crawled out from under the car and sat up. He peered toward the ramp at the end of the building, wondering what could be waiting for him above.

Curiosity finally got the best of him, and he climbed back over the partition. He held the lantern out in front of him as he slowly walked up the steep, curving ramp. Slowly, the upper floor came into view, and he found that his suspicions were correct. The upper level, like the ground floor, was also crammed full of cars.

These vehicles were distinctively different from the others; they were sleeker, and not as rounded as the ones below. Matt started to see some familiar-looking shapes. The numbers on the plaques, he noticed, were getting higher. He read the nearest one, which was placed in front of a bright orange car adorned with a flag on the roof.

"1969 Dodge Charger," he read aloud.

He nodded with approval and resumed walking. The floor crunched loudly beneath his feet. He looked down and saw tiny bones amongst the white crust of bird droppings. He raised the lantern again to resume his inspection.

A loud screech pierced the night, and the beating of great wings drove Matt to the floor. A shape soared over his head, and he looked up in time to catch a glimpse of feathers as the shape exited through a hole in the corner of the roof.

"Owl," he breathed. "Shit."

He wiped the sheen of sweat from his brow. As he turned to stand, something behind the Plexiglas caught his eye. He held the lantern up to the clear partition. There, affixed to the grill of the nearest car, was a three-dimensional rendering of a strange bird with a bright yellow beak, big white eyes, and a plume of purple feathers on its head.

The car before Matt was the most beautiful thing he had ever seen. It was bright yellow, sat low to the ground, had two doors, and black stripes leading from the roof down the quarter panels. The Air Grabber hood and oddly shaped nose seemed to scream silently, begging for release. For speed.

He blew the dust from the plaque, and reverently read the words etched into it, "1971 Plymouth Road Runner."

Road Runner. Even the name implied "speed."

ADAM J. WHITLATCH

Matt looked at the Road Runner and nodded. "Bingo."

# Five

Keys. Where were the goddamned keys? Matt had searched every inch of the building, and all he'd found was dust and mouse turds. They had to be in another building, but which one? He stalked through the courtyard and came to a large building, by far the biggest in the entire resort. He tried the doorknob and found it to be unlocked. Holding the lantern aloft, he stepped into the gloom.

Beyond the door, he found a rare treasure, indeed - a vending machine filled with bottled water. He set the lantern down and kicked the glass front, shattering it into a thousand tiny shards. He grabbed as many of the bottles as would fit into his pack, amazed that the machine was still half full. He decided to come back for the rest later and moved on.

The building was cluttered with miscellaneous household items, with only enough room for two men to walk abreast amongst the rows. This building, like the first, was obviously some kind of museum; it wasn't likely he would find the keys in here. He navigated the twisting rows of washing machines, radios and other appliances until he came to a corridor that set him on edge.

The hall was long, stretching into the inky blackness, possibly all the way to the other side of the building. Lining the walkway were Plexiglas windows taller than a person. The flickering light of the lantern cast strange shapes across the bowed windows. Matt stepped into the corridor and held his lantern up to one of the windows.

Behind it was a room. It had log walls, a dirt floor, and a stone hearth. Rough, stick-built furniture sat collecting dust.

"What the hell?" Matt whispered.

He turned, and immediately something in the lamplight caught his eye. Through the gloom, he could distinctly make out a smiling face staring back at him. He gave a startled shout and drew the Well Digger from its holster. He fired a wild shot in the direction of the face and - in the brief flash of the blast - he thought he could make out more faces in the room beyond.

The shot echoed throughout the building, followed by the beating of wings as dozens of birds and bats were roused from their slumber. Matt's arm remained stiff, waiting for the slightest movement behind the window, but there was none. Slowly, he shuffled up to it and looked through the ragged bullet hole. A mannequin dressed in a blue dress, white apron, and missing the left half of its head held out a tray of plastic cookies.

Behind the dummy were three others. One, a male, sat in a red chair with a curled yellow newspaper in its hands and a pipe jutting from its mouth. The others, a small boy and girl, lay on an oval rug smiling up at a dark and silent wooden radio. Matt lowered his gun, and a short laugh burst from his lips. He laughed louder as he holstered the weapon.

Another stupid exhibit.

A plaque similar to the ones in the car building was mounted to the wall next to the window. Matt held up his lantern. It read, "Typical American Living Room - 1940s."

There were more just like it. One side of the aisle showed more primitive dwellings, which became more advanced as he walked; the same could be said for the other side. Spinning wheels gave way to sewing machines and radios were replaced by television sets. There were living rooms, bedrooms, and kitchens; most of them were populated with smiling dummies.

Matt marveled at these sights - preserved dioramas of life before the war, when water flowed freely from pipes in the walls and food came in bright, vacuum-sealed packages. When ice cubes clinked in glasses on even the hottest summer days. These were things his grandfather had told him about on cold nights by the fire, things no man had seen in over forty years.

Oh, rooms like these still existed, but so worn down by the elements and time to be almost unrecognizable when compared to these wonders. Televisions became fireplaces. Refrigerators became coffins. This world - the world of his grandfather - was long gone. And this was all that remained of it.

As he passed the 1980s kitchen, with its microwave and food processors, Matt came upon a bright yellow metal sign with black markings - markings he'd come to know all too well in his travels. The sign read "Fallout Shelter," and above these words, the universal warning sign for nuclear radiation. A yellow Geiger counter - much like the one stowed in his pack - hung below.

He held the lantern up to the window and looked in. What he saw chilled him to the bone. Cinder block walls encased another family of grinning mannequins. The children sat playing cards on top of a bunk bed while their father stood counting row after row of aluminum food cans and the mother rocked an infant in a chair near the corner.

"They knew," Matt whispered.

He stared at the dumb smiling faces and felt his blood begin to boil.

"They fucking *knew!*"

He kicked the window, and the Plexiglas wobbled.

He kicked again, and spit flew from his lips. "They fucking knew! They knew what would fucking happen!"

The window cracked and bowed inward under his boot. He forced his way inside and punched the father dummy in the face, toppling it and sending the head rolling underneath the bunk beds. He swept his arm across one of the shelves, and the cans - empty and opened from the bottom - clattered to the floor with a hollow, mocking sound.

He threw his head back and screamed, his voice echoing back at him from every corner. They'd had it all. Before the war, they'd had everything; they built it from dirt and wood, but what they left behind was a legacy of rust and ash. Life was good... and they'd thrown it all away.

"For what?" Matt asked the mannequins. "Huh? *What for?*"

Silence.

He shook his head and drew a deep, rattling breath. He had to get out of here - out of this building, out of this town, out of this butt-ugly flat state. The sooner he found those keys and pointed the Road Runner east, the better. He stepped back into the corridor and ran into the darkness, searching for the door.

When he finally found the exit, there was a map hanging next to it. He scanned it until he found the words he was looking for: WELCOME CENTER/OFFICE. He tore the map off the wall and kicked open the door. He ran into the night, away from the museum and the ignorant, smiling ghosts of the past.

*****

He found the keys to the Road Runner in a lockbox hanging on the wall in the office. The welcome center contained two more vending machines like the one in the museum, and he emptied their contents into a couple canvas tote bags from the gift shop. He dragged the heavy sacks briskly past the Model T Fords, stuffed animals and underneath the replica of the Wright Brothers' airplane, anxious to be out of this place and back on the open road where he felt safest.

He bypassed the other buildings on the way back to the car museum, not caring to learn any more about the world stolen from him. There was no time anyway. Once those pirates found him, his goose would be thoroughly cooked. He could hear the sound of engines carried on the wind whistling between the buildings.

Or was that his imagination?

*Run, Mattie*, a voice in the back of his mind whispered. *Run!*

Back in the car museum, he dropped his bounty and went to the Jeep. He removed the jack from under the passenger seat, tucked one of the car batteries under his arm and grabbed a toolbox. He took these up to the second level and made another trip for a gas can and bicycle pump.

The first order of business was to ensure the Road Runner would even start. If not, then he'd have to find another car that would. If none of them would - well, he didn't even want to think about that possibility. He lifted the hood and took his first look at the engine. He whistled; four letters printed on the air filter cover made all of the effort to resurrect this beast worth it:

H E M I

"All right," he whispered. "Let's get to work."

The first thing was the battery, which, as he expected, the car was lacking. Then he probed the nooks and crannies of the engine, removing mouse nests wherever he could reach them. He checked to ensure all of the hoses and belts were present and intact; they were. But when he squeezed the coolant hose, a horrible thought came to mind.

Coolant.

He unscrewed the radiator cap and shone his lantern down into the hole. Bone dry. Of course. Why wouldn't it be?

Matt took a step back and considered his situation. Suddenly, he remembered the tote bags filled with bottled water at the bottom of the ramp and went to retrieve them. He picked up one of the bottles and unscrewed the cap. For the second time that day, he found himself pouring an obscene amount of water down into a radiator. He hoped this time the outcome would be better.

"Christ, you're an expensive whore," he said as he dumped the fifteenth bottle into the radiator.

Not wanting to waste gas, he removed the air filter to expose the carburetor. He carefully poured a small amount of gasoline down into the barrels. The risk of ignition and back flash was great, but it beat the alternative. With time growing short, he was willing to take the chance.

He opened the driver's side door and sat down. The seat was leather, and very comfortable. He pulled the key out of his pocket and inserted it into the ignition. He mouthed a silent prayer and turned it.

To his relief, the starter turned, but the engine would not turn over. He tried the key again, but the disheartening *URR-R-R-R* coming from under the hood wasn't promising. He got out and looked from the carburetor to the gas can.

"Please," he whispered as he dumped another half a cup of gas down into the carburetor. *"Pleasepleaseplease!"*

He sat back down in the driver's seat and turned the key. The result was the same. He squeezed his eyes shut and turned the key again. To his elation, the HEMI came to life with a roar that shook the entire building. He shouted in triumph as the engine shuddered and died, its fuel source exhausted.

The Road Runner would live again.

He slumped back in the seat and breathed a sigh of relief. His luck, such as it was, was holding. But soon the pirates would be descending on him like a dust storm, and he might have to fight his way out. He got out of the car and shut the door. There was work to do.

He stripped the Jeep of everything he considered useful, and then siphoned the remaining gas and drained the oil, which he then transferred to the Road Runner. The tires were the worst part. It took him the better part of an hour to inflate all four with the pathetic bicycle pump, and when he finished, he slumped back against the door, exhausted.

The weller closed his eyes and took a deep breath. He was asleep before his chin touched his chest.

# Six

Young Mattie Freeborn watched as his grandfather, Gene, wiped a bead of sweat from his forehead and sucked the salty liquid from his finger. The old man smiled at the boy and resumed reeling in the line that vanished into the hole at their feet. Gene peered down into the gloom of the well, watching for any sign of the bucket. Finally, its vague outline slowly rose into view; the water inside sparkled enticingly as it caught a glint of the noonday sun.

A large shadow passed over them, blotting out the blistering Arizona sun momentarily. Gene looked up at the flock of buzzards circling overhead waiting for their next meal and smiled humorlessly. The bastards would have to go hungry. No free lunch today.

"I don't like the look of those things, Grandpa," said Mattie. "They keep gettin' closer."

Gene hefted the heavy bucket out of the well and placed it carefully onto the cracked earth. He turned to look at the ginger-haired youth of about fifteen and smiled.

"Heh," Gene chuckled and reached into his tattered traveling cloak. "You ever seen what this thing can do to a buzzard, Mattie?"

Mattie's eyes grew wide with anticipation as his grandfather drew his most prized possession. The boy had only seen Gene fire the Well Digger twice, once at a drunken road pirate who had foolishly accused the old weller of stealing from him, and once into the back of the man who had killed the boy's father three years before.

Gene raised the Well Digger with one wiry arm, his other hand shielding his eyes from the desert glare. "Watch this."

Mattie's eyes darted between the hand-cannon in his grandfather's hand and the circling carrion-eaters above. Gene took careful aim and squeezed the trigger. A flash of flame spat from both barrels. The weapon's report sounded like a blast of thunder, the wrath of the gods themselves. The recoil would have felled a lesser man, but it was common knowledge in these parts that Gene Freeborn was not a lesser man.

Mattie clamped his hands over his ears and looked up expectantly at the flock of buzzards. There was a pregnant moment of anticipation, then one of the dark shapes exploded into a cloud of red mist and fluttering feathers. Ragged chunks of flesh splattered the cracked, dusty ground like some hellish Old Testament rain. A small chunk landed at the wellers' feet with a disgusting, wet *plop*.

Mattie stared down at it for a moment before meeting his grandfather's gaze with a toothy grin. "Cool."

Gene smiled as he slipped the gun back into the holster beneath his cloak. "Them buzzards won't be bothering us anytime soon, Mattie. They'll be busy cleaning up after their friend."

Mattie wrinkled his nose as the birds began to change course and circle the "carcass" of their fallen comrade. "Eww."

Gene turned his attention back to the bucket and carefully filled a yellowed plastic vial with water. Mattie watched intently as his grandfather filled a medicine dropper with liquid from a small, amber-tinted bottle and carefully squeezed two drops into the vial. He swirled the water gently, and after a few moments, the water inside the vial turned a very light purple. Gene grunted his approval.

He dumped the vial onto the ground, which greedily sucked up the wet offering. "So far so good, Mattie."

Mattie's eyes widened expectantly. "Think we found a good well, Grandpa? Are we gonna be rich?"

Gene's expression became serious. "Wellers have no business bein' rich, Mattie. My pa always told me to never trust a preacher or a carpenter that drives a Cadillac. Same goes for wellers."

"What's a Cadillac?"

Gene smiled. "Hand me the clicker, boy."

"Yes'ir." Mattie rummaged through the bag at his knees until he pulled out a battered Geiger counter. "Here you go, Grandpa."

Gene took the device and turned it on. Many a find had been spoiled by a spastically chattering clicker; water ruined by the lingering radiation of the bombs dropped during the Twelve-Minute War. The machine chattered furiously for half a second before calming down to a quiet clicking. Gene took the wand and waved it slowly over the bucket, but the machine's sound never changed and the needle gave only the tiniest of jerks.

A wide grin slowly spread across his sun-darkened features as he turned to his grandson. "Mattie, we've finally done it."

"We found the mother lode?" Mattie jumped to his feet.

Gene nodded and placed the Geiger counter back in the bag. "Go fetch the jugs. We'll have to boil it to make sure there ain't any bugs in it, but I have a feeling we're in the clear."

Mattie whooped as he turned to run for the Jeep. They'd be able to afford lots of things now. With this water, they could buy supplies in Resurrection City - and maybe even a bath! With *soap*! He tried to remember the last time he had a nice hot bath. Was it his thirteenth birthday? Had it really been that long?

He reached into the back of the Jeep, threw the dusty blue tarp aside and began tossing plastic jugs of varying sizes and colors over his shoulder. As he stood tiptoed to reach for the last jug, he heard a metallic *thunk*. He looked over his shoulder and saw a rusty steel arrow imbedded in the door next to him. The arrow's arrival was accompanied by a loud and unsettling cry from the desert.

Mattie jumped out of the Jeep and scanned the desert. His eyes fought against the harsh glare of the sun until he barely caught a glimpse of a silhouette ducking down behind a boulder.

He pointed toward the rock. "Grandpa!"

"I seen him," Gene answered, reaching into his cloak for the Well Digger.

With another wild whoop, the distant assailant darted out from behind the boulder and fired another poorly aimed shot at the old weller. The arrow struck the bucket and passed almost completely through before the tail lodged in the wood. Water trickled down the side and onto the parched earth. Gene scowled and took careful aim at the edge of the boulder, waiting for the assailant to poke his head out again.

"Cowardly desert rats," he snarled.

Moments later, the figure appeared from behind the rock and Gene could make out a crossbow clutched in the attacker's hands, but the weller's reflexes were quicker, and he squeezed the trigger. The Well Digger's report echoed through the valley as a sizable chunk of the boulder vaporized into a cloud of orange dust, missing the target by mere inches. Gene cursed and adjusted his aim, determined to turn the assassin into a wet, red stain on the side of the rock.

As he prepared to pull the trigger a second time, an arrow whistled through the air from the direction of the cliffs to his right and passed through the thick muscle of his forearm. He stared in shock at the arrow as his fingers went numb and the Well Digger fell to the ground.

Mattie dashed to his grandfather's aid. "Grandpa!"

"*Wooooooo!*" came a triumphant yell from behind the boulder as Mattie's would-be assassin abandoned his hiding place. "You got 'im, Pa! You got 'im!"

At the sight of the man, Mattie came to a skidding halt, his boots sliding in the dust. The man with the crossbow was as misshapen a monster as anything the boy's imagination could ever conjure up - worse even. A large three-headed lump protruded from his forehead, partially covering one of his large, yellow-tinged eyes. His nose was not only large and bulbous, but also hopelessly lopsided. Two of the fingers on his right hand were fused together into one thick digit that shared one chunky, cracked fingernail.

*Mutants.*

Matt had always heard stories about mutants; disfigured, inbred freaks that crawled out of the radioactive ruins of Old Phoenix after the food and water supplies had been exhausted. When she was still alive, Mattie's mother had told stories about cannibals who would snatch infants from their cribs during the night, favoring the meat as the most tender and sweetest of all delicacies. Sometimes they even took the mothers for "fresh blood." The stories had given him nightmares, and now he saw his most vivid nightmare come to life - and it was aiming a crossbow at his grandfather.

"Run, Mattie," Gene shouted, snapping the boy out of his trance. "Run!"

Mattie whirled and ran for the Jeep, his boots slipping on the loose sand peppering the hard earth. He lunged over the door and reached for the battered .22 rifle nestled between the front seats. He cursed as the barrel became entangled in the seatbelt. He could hear uneven footfalls behind him and knew that one of the mutants must be drawing near.

Finally the rifle came loose, and Mattie whirled, bringing the barrel across the attacking mutant's face. The freak howled and recoiled as the sight ripped a gash across his temple. Mattie fumbled the rifle as he chambered a round. When the mutant came back up to attack, he grabbed the barrel and tried to wrench the rifle from the boy's grasp. Mattie screamed and pulled the trigger.

The mutant gasped as the bullet tore through its stomach, and looked down to stare at the tiny bleeding wound. The mutant shrieked with rage as it released the smoking weapon and brought both arms up to strike Mattie. The young weller apprentice did not hesitate; he brought the rifle up and fired again, this time through the mutant's grime-encrusted throat. The mutant clutched its neck and slowly fell to the ground at Mattie's feet.

As the mutant fell, Mattie saw a second mutant wielding a sling. The freak swung it and loosed a rock at the young weller's head, but Mattie ducked, and the stone sailed harmlessly over the Jeep. Mattie snapped the butt of the rifle up to his shoulder and leveled his sight on the mutant's grotesque face.

"Hold it right there, mister," the boy shouted. "Or I'll put one right between your eyes!"

The mutant laughed. It was a hysterical, stupid sound. "Betcha ya can't!"

The mutant raised the sling and began to swing, but unfortunately for him, Mattie was true to his word and fired. The shot went wide, however, and took a sizable chunk of the mutant's right ear off. Mattie cursed and chambered another round, but his finger came off the trigger as the thunderous report of the Well Digger echoed through the valley and a voice called out.

"I wouldn't do that if I were you, boy," said the voice.

Mattie craned his neck to look over the shoulder of the sling-wielding mutant and gasped. Gene lay on the ground, a thick rope net wrapped around his writhing body. A man stood over him with the Well Digger pointed at Gene's head. This man appeared less misshapen than the others, but was so scraggly that Mattie really couldn't tell under all that hair.

Mattie shifted his aim and focused on the man holding his grandfather hostage. This was exactly the distraction the mutant with the sling needed, and he loosed another rock at Mattie. The stone struck the boy on the side of his head, cutting a deep gash into his scalp and sending him reeling to the desert floor.

"Mattie!" Gene reached for his fallen kin, his outstretched fingers poking through the holes in the net.

Gene's captor knelt beside him and traced the Well Digger's double barrels along the weller's jaw line. The man leaned in close and inhaled deeply, savoring the old weller's scent like some pre-war Thanksgiving feast.

"I like weller meat," the man said with a stinking, jagged-toothed smile. "Weller meat's *moist*."

This brought howls of laughter from the other two mutants. Gene grimaced and spat in the man's face.

"How's that for moist?" he snarled.

The last thing Gene saw before the world went dark was the butt of the Well Digger coming straight for the side of his face.

# Seven

Mattie woke to the sound of screams, followed by raucous, hooting laughter. His head felt like it was splitting apart. He tried to sit up but could not move his arms; they were bound behind his back with rope. When he raised his head and opened his eyes, the room began to spin violently. Vertigo overtook him, and he vomited.

The screams and laughter continued, but while the laughter grew louder with each passing moment, the screams slowly ebbed into pained whimpers. Where was he? His mind was muddled, foggy. He was indoors, that much he knew. The human funk was overpowering.

He remembered the buzzard. His ears still rang slightly from the Well Digger's discharge. But his grandfather had fired more than one shot. Who had he been shooting at?

A loud, stupid voice reverberated through the wall. "Good one, Pa!"

*The mutants!*

Mattie opened his eyes. He was in a small, cluttered room. The walls were wooden planks, like the floor. He was in a shack, and a poorly constructed one at that. Three of the walls had large gaps where sunlight shone through. Dusty deer heads and stuffed birds adorned the walls.

In one dark corner, Mattie noticed a large pile of discarded shoes of all sizes and styles. One pair that stuck out to him more than the others was a pair of red, white and blue toddlers' sneakers. He tried his best to keep his mind off the possibilities of what fate the sneakers' owner might have met, but despite his best efforts, he felt what little remained of his lunch rising up into his throat, and another wave of vomit spewed from his mouth.

The screams erupted again from the adjoining room, and he recognized the anguished voice of his grandfather. Renewed howls of laughter joined the chorus, along with jeering yells of "Hold 'im steady!" and "Quit squirmin', weller!"

"Grandpa!" Mattie shouted.

He tried to rise to his feet, but the top of his head struck the bottom of a solid wooden workbench, and his vision exploded into a field of popping stars. He winced and tears stung his eyes as he instinctively tried to rub his head, but his bound wrists did not budge. His outburst brought the mutants; the first through the door was the one-eared mutant he'd shot out in the wastes. The freak grinned at him as he hunched down to taunt him.

"Well now," said the mutant. "Lookie what we have here! Good morning, Sunshine."

"Yeah," said the other. "Wakie wakie, eggs and bakie."

"Lincoln!" barked a gruff voice from the next room. "What the hell is going on in there?"

"The pup's awake, Pa!" replied the mutant with the wounded ear.

"Better make sure he's tied tight, Link," said the other mutant with a sneer. "Don't want 'im takin' your other ear off, or worse, do you like he did poor Edsel!"

Lincoln punched his brother in the shoulder. "Shut up, Mercury!"

Mercury punched back. Soon the two grotesque brothers began rolling on the floor, punching, head-butting and kneeing each other to a bruised pulp.

A deafening gunshot split the air, and the two brothers came to a startled halt, scrambling over each other to face the door. There,

40

framed in the doorway, stood the man Mattie had seen in the desert; the hairy man. From this distance, he could see now that he was even uglier than he could ever have perceived.

The man's left eye was white and dead in its socket. His face was riddled with deep pockmarks, and his skin was shiny with oil. His beard was thick, black and hopelessly tangled; forgotten bits of food and debris littered the mat of hair. In his filthy, upraised hand, he held the Well Digger. Mattie's eyes wandered from the smoking barrels to the large, jagged hole in the tin roof. The man grinned like a child with a new toy.

Mercury hooted with laughter as he staggered to his feet. "Damn, Pa! You 'bout scared the bejesus outta me."

The bearded man smirked. "Boys, go fetch that old weller and make him nice an' comfy."

"You got it, Pa," the mutants said in unison, scrambling for the door and leaving Mattie alone with the gun-toting terror.

The man knelt in front of Mattie. "Name's Ford. What's yours?"

Mattie didn't answer, opting instead to spit in the man's filthy face.

Ford pressed Well Digger against Mattie's temple. "Boy, you two are the most *wastenest* damn wellers I have *ever* met in my entire life!"

Mattie grimaced at Ford. Sweat streamed down his face as the Well Digger's hot barrels dug into his skin. He breathed hard through his nose, nostrils flared like a cornered animal.

"That's okay," Ford said. "I don't need to know your name to enjoy your meat. I think I'll eat the meat off your finger bones first. Hell, I might even make you try some yourself while you're still squirmin'. What d'ya say, boy?"

Mattie never had a chance to answer, because at that moment Lincoln and Mercury returned with Gene, who was no longer struggling and looked alarmingly pale. The old weller's arms were slung over the mutants' shoulders. Mattie's eyes grew wide as saucers as the mutants carried his grandfather past him - Gene's left leg was severed at the top of the thigh. The stench of burning flesh stung Mattie's nostrils.

41

The mutants had removed his grandfather's leg and cauterized the wound.

"Grandpa!" Mattie shouted.

Gene's only reply was a weakened moan.

Mattie watched, helpless, as the two deformed hillbillies dragged Gene to the opposite wall.

"Now, boys, you be careful with him," Ford shouted. "Boys! No, boys, d—"

The mutants laughed as they lifted Gene by the arms and heaved his body onto a rusty meat hook hanging from the wall. The sickening sound of steel penetrating flesh and bone reached Mattie's ears, even through Pa Ford's angry shouts. Mattie's bottom lip quivered in shock as he watched his grandfather spasm violently, hanging by his back. Gene screamed and flailed his arms, vainly trying to reach the hook and free himself.

*"Grandpa!"* Mattie shrieked.

"You shit-fer-brains!" Ford snarled and slapped Lincoln's wounded ear. "I told you to be careful! Don't you still got one good ear to listen with?"

"Ow, Pa," Lincoln whined and cupped his throbbing ear. "What's the big deal?"

"Yeah," Mercury chimed in. "We're just gonna wind up cuttin' him up anyway."

"Stupid!" spat Ford. "Maybe I didn't want a pantry stocked with nothing but *jerky*, didja ever think of that?"

Mattie couldn't believe his ears. They were actually discussing cutting his grandfather into pieces and *eating* him. Of course Mattie understood cannibalism, what child in the wastes didn't? But to actually be experiencing it firsthand was unthinkable.

"We still got the boy, Pa," Mercury said. "This ol' buzzard's too tough to be good for anything but jerky anyways."

Ford glanced over his shoulder at Mattie and sneered. "You do make a good point, Mercury."

"So what do you wanna do, Pa?" asked Lincoln.

"First we eat," Ford grinned. "Then we make weller jerky."

The mutants laughed and ran to the door.

Ford turned to face Mattie. "Now don't you go nowhere. We have a dinner date."

Mattie turned away to hide the tears in his eyes as the cannibal slammed the door. He heard the sound of a padlock being fastened on the other side. When he looked up, his grandfather's eyes were closed, and his chin rested against his chest.

"Grandpa?" Mattie whispered.

Gene was silent and still.

Mattie got to his knees and walked awkwardly across the floor to where the old man hung. His breathing was labored with sickness and sobs of grief. Gently, he rested his cheek against his grandfather's remaining thigh.

"Grandpa!" the boy sobbed.

Gene's fingers twitched and weakly caressed the boy's hair. Mattie jumped and looked up at his grandfather.

"Mattie," the old man croaked, his throat raw from screaming and thirst.

"I'm here, Grandpa!"

"Listen to me, Mattie," he rasped. "I want you to run."

"But, Grandpa, I'm all tied up."

Gene nodded. "You're a smart boy, Mattie. I know you'll find a way."

Mattie shook his head. "I won't leave you, Grandpa!"

"Damn it, boy, you'll do as you're told!"

Mattie sobbed and hung his head, his bottom lip quivering. His grandfather had only raised his voice to him once in his entire life, and that had been when he had stolen rock candy from a general store in Resurrection City when he was eight years old.

Again, Gene's fingers stroked Mattie's ginger locks. When he spoke, his voice seemed to regain some of its vigor and tone; the same voice that Mattie would fall asleep listening to as the old man told him stories of the world long before the bombs fell.

"Ain't no shame in running, Mattie. Remember what I told you about knowing when to cut your losses?"

Mattie nodded.

"Your daddy never learned that lesson," said Gene, "and you saw where that got him, didn't you?"

Mattie sniffled. "Yes'ir."

"First chance you get," Gene said, his voice beginning to fade. "I want you to run for the Jeep and make for the hills. Don't you *ever* look back, you hear me?"

"Yes, Grandpa."

"Good boy." Gene winced. "Now you go on and mind your old gramps, y'hear?"

Mattie nodded and blinked his eyes. "But, Grandpa, what about you?"

Silence.

"Grandpa?"

Mattie looked up into Gene's open, sightless eyes. The boy panicked and stood, his eyes chest level with his elder. He looked up into those eyes and cried as he fought against his bonds.

"Grandpa!" he shrieked, knowing the truth, but unwilling to accept it. "*Grandpa!*"

The door leading to the other room rattled violently and Mattie jumped away from the body, startled. The door didn't open. Instead, Mercury's muffled voice called out from the other side.

"You shut the hell up in there," the mutant commanded. "Quit yer wailin'!"

Mattie fell and scuttled back against the wall, putting as much distance between himself and the door as possible. Something sharp bit into his palm and he winced. He turned and saw that he had backed right into a smashed kerosene lantern, the glass broken into jagged tooth-like shards. One of the points was coated in blood, and he watched as a fat, red drop fell to the dusty floor.

He scanned the floorboards, looking for the largest shard he could find, and then he spotted it, diamond-shaped and almost three inches long. He searched with his hands and took it between his fingers, awkwardly positioning the edge against the rope binding his wrists. Slowly, he sawed at his bindings. He bit his lip to keep from crying out every time he slipped and nicked his palm. Gradually, he felt the bonds loosen, until he could almost slip his hand through the loop.

Finally the glass cut through the last bit of rope and Mattie's hands flew apart. For a moment, he could only rub his aching wrists and shoulders, and then he went about the task of plotting his escape. He scanned the floor for any loose boards or holes large enough to crawl through, but there were none. The walls were too sturdy to break through, and besides, the noise would surely bring the mutants running.

A sunbeam stung his eyes, and he lifted his hand to shield his vision. Then he stopped and slowly lowered his guard. He followed the sunbeam all the way up to the tin ceiling above his head. He noticed one of the metal sheets was loose and slightly bent.

He hopped up onto the workbench, reached for the top of the wall and slipped his fingers under the metal. The ceiling panel lifted easily away from the wall.

He was free.

He climbed from the table to a shelf and slung his leg over the top of the wall, careful not to catch himself on a protruding nail. He paused to look back at his grandfather's limp body. For a moment, he considered going back to close the old man's eyes, but then thought better of it. Gene would have scolded him for such foolishness when freedom was so close.

"Goodbye, Grandpa," he whispered.

He turned and jumped down to the sandy ground below. When he landed, he twisted his ankle, which sent him rolling. His mouth opened in a silent scream as he cradled the injured foot. Slowly, he got to his feet and tested his ankle; it hurt, but could support him well enough to walk.

The Jeep was parked only twenty feet away; he could make it. His boots slipped on the loose sand as he hopped toward the vehicle. When he reached the Jeep, he felt under the rear bumper, searching for the spare key. Finally his fingers brushed the frayed duct tape, and he tore the key from its hiding spot. He limped to the driver's side.

He carefully opened the door and settled into the seat, fidgeting with the key and fumbling it several times in his numb fingers as he tried to force it into the ignition. Finally it slid home. Mattie paused.

He turned his head toward the rundown shack. For a moment he only stared, but then - without taking his eyes off it - he opened the door and stepped out of the Jeep.

His boots crunched on the sand and loose gravel as he limped to the rear of the vehicle, his sore ankle burning with every step. He reached into the back and tore off the tarp, revealing several tools, empty water jars, and a rust-spotted tire iron. As he looked down at the tool, his grandfather's final words rang in his ears.

*"Ain't no shame in running, Mattie,"* the old man had said.

"Sorry, Grandpa," Mattie said as his fingers wrapped around the cold steel shaft. "Not this time."

He hefted the tire iron in his hand and turned toward the house, finding each step progressively easier than the last, despite the pain in his ankle. As the house grew nearer, he felt his grief and rage growing into a thunderhead. At that moment, young Mattie Freeborn became a force of nature. He placed his hand against the rickety wooden door and pushed slowly, making as little noise as possible.

Bit by bit, the main room of the shack came into view, and he could see the mutants inside, silhouetted against the cooking fire as they sat at their table eating. He noticed the empty chair that would have been occupied by Edsel, had the mutant not fallen by his hand, and felt a sense of grim satisfaction.

Silently, he slipped into the house and made his way across the floor. The smell of cooking meat filled the air, and he noticed the large hunk of flesh roasting on a spit over the fire: his grandfather's left leg. This brought his wrath to a level he could never have imagined, and he raised the tire iron as he approached the nearest mutant from behind.

At that moment, his boot found a loose squeaky board, and the mutant turned in time to see the tire iron come down hard on his face. Mattie didn't flinch as Lincoln's blood splashed onto his cheeks and brought the weapon around for another blow, this time driving the tool's pointed end through what remained of the mutant's left ear. The other cannibals, their reflexes slowed by their gorged stomachs, didn't turn until they heard the sound of Lincoln's twitching corpse hitting the floor.

Mercury clumsily got to his feet, sending the table and what was left of their meal clattering to the floor. The mutant reached for the Bowie knife sheathed to his hip, but Mattie lunged forward and pushed him into the fire. The mutant shrieked and flailed as he got to his feet and ran about the room, knocking trinkets from the walls as he tried to extinguish his flaming clothes. Mattie raised the bloody tire iron to finish the mutant off, but Mercury's arm lashed out and struck him on the nose, sending the boy sprawling to the floor.

Mattie shook his head, trying to clear his vision, and for a moment, he thought he was seeing things, because there on the floor in front of him was the Well Digger. He reached out and grabbed it. The revolver felt unbelievably heavy in his hand; he had never held the weapon before in his entire life.

The room became brighter as Mercury's rampage lit every piece of combustible flotsam in the shack. With his clothes finally extinguished, the mutant glared at the boy, his ugliness only worsened by his singed eyebrows and blistered skin. Mattie saw the bloody machete in the mutant's hand and raised the Well Digger in both of his, aiming the massive weapon right between Mercury's eyes.

The mutant howled and charged Mattie, machete raised. Mattie squeezed back on the trigger, and the Well Digger recoiled, kicking back in his weak grip and striking him on the forehead. The impact sent him reeling to the floor. He never saw Mercury's head explode into a cloud of red mist through the stars dancing across his vision and blood dripping from the deep gash in his forehead.

He felt along the ground for the Well Digger, but instead of finding it, he heard it. Somewhere behind and above him, he heard the hammer cock back and the cylinder cycle into position. Blistering hot steel seared the top of his head as the barrels of his family's prized weapon pressed hard against his skull. He strained to look up and saw the furious eye of Pa Ford glaring down upon him.

"You little son of a bitch," the cannibal snarled. "You killed my boys!"

Smoke began to fill the room, and Mattie's eyes began to sting and tear up.

"Mama always told me not to play with my food," Ford said as he squeezed the trigger, "but I'm really gonna enjoy playing with *you*, you little bastard."

Mattie squeezed his eyes shut. He took some small degree of comfort knowing that he wouldn't even feel it. The Well Digger was merciful if nothing else.

*Click.*

Mattie's eyes snapped open. Ford pulled back the hammer and pulled the trigger again, but again both chambers were empty. Mattie rolled away from Ford and crawled below the smoke to where Mercury lay next to the cooking fire. He wrenched the machete from the mutant's stiff fingers and turned to face Ford, who was still cycling through the chambers with a bewildered look on his face.

"Forget to reload, Ford?" Mattie said, his voice cold and unsympathetic.

Ford threw down the gun and held out his arms to protect himself as the boy stalked toward him. Mattie brought the machete down hard on Ford's shoulder, cleaving through muscle and bone. The cannibal screamed as he saw the fires of Hell reflected in Mattie's eyes.

"Are you having fun yet, Ford?"

The cannibal gave a gurgling cry as Mattie wrenched the blade from his shoulder and brought it around for the killing stroke. The machete cut clean through to the bone, and Pa Ford's head rolled away into the rising flames.

"Because I sure am," Mattie intoned as he knelt to retrieve the Well Digger.

Gun in hand, and the machete hanging loosely from the other, he stepped over Ford's body and slowly limped through the front door. Once outside, he reveled in how cool and clean the blistering desert air felt compared to the heat and stench of the burning shack.

As he approached the Jeep, he turned to look back at the burning shack in time to see the roof cave in.

He felt a pang of regret in his gut as he thought of his grandfather - he would not have wanted to be buried with this pack of desert rats - but then the old man's words came back to him once again as he watched the thick black smoke rise high into the sky.

*"First chance you get, I want you to run for the Jeep and make for the hills. Don't you ever look back, you hear me?"*

As Mattie climbed into the Jeep, he tossed the bloody machete into the back and placed the Well Digger reverently on the seat next to him. He stared down at it for a moment and turned the key. The engine roared to life, and he put the vehicle in gear. He pointed the Jeep east and adjusted the rearview mirror so that he couldn't see the plumes of smoke rising behind him.

"Never look back," he whispered.

He put the accelerator to the floor, perfectly content to follow that final piece of advice. That day, he'd learned the harshest of lessons, that there was no easy way out of the wastelands. The only way out was no different than any other birth: kicking, screaming, and covered in blood.

# Eight

Matt woke with a start. He blinked his eyes and yawned. Then he heard it - it was faint at first, but growing more distinct with every passing second.

Engines. Lots of them.

He jumped to his feet and scrambled to load the rest of his tools into the Road Runner. He'd already dismantled the partition, so there was nothing stopping him from leaving with his prize - except the Jeep. It still sat inside the door, blocking his escape route.

He drove the Road Runner down the ramp and parked it. He crept around the Jeep and looked through a slit in the door. A single pirate vehicle turned down a side street several blocks away. He looked down at the puddle of oil inside the gate, and the small but distinct trail leading out into the street. Soon they would find it and trace him here, where he was cornered.

Unless...

Matt grinned and ran back to the Road Runner's open trunk. He reached in and pulled out a red five-gallon gas can. He shook it; about two gallons of gasoline sloshed inside. It wasn't a lot, but it would do the trick.

He poured most of it into the Jeep's tank, saving some of the precious fuel. Then he inched the massive sliding door on the building open, stopping to hold his breath and listen every time the rusty metal screeched. When it was wide enough to let the Jeep through, he pushed the dead vehicle out into the cold night air. He rolled it over the puddle of oil where it had died and set the parking brake.

He retrieved the almost-empty gas can and poured a thin line of fuel from beneath the Jeep's tank up to the building's entrance. The sound of roaring engines was growing louder, and suddenly the Jeep was illuminated from behind him, leaving his black silhouette against the side. He turned and saw one of the pirate vehicles at the end of the street.

"I found 'im!" the driver shouted, laying on his horn.

Matt dug into his coat pocket and pulled out a straight-bladed screwdriver. He crawled underneath the Jeep and, careful not to get any gasoline on him, punched it in the side of the tank near the bottom. A slow trickle of gas drizzled through the ragged hole.

Matt rolled out from under the Jeep. As the pirate vehicle approached, he ran back to the building, scooping up the empty gas can as he crossed the threshold.

He threw the can into the Road Runner's trunk and slammed it shut; no sense in trying to be stealthy now. The Road Runner was parked at the back of the building, deep in the shadows. To the pirates gathering outside, he was invisible. There was nothing to do now but wait for the entire gang to show up. Then the party could get under way.

A smirk crept across Matt's lips as he twirled the screwdriver in his left hand... and fingered the piece of flint in his right pocket.

*****

The leader of the pirates steered his Crown Victoria toward the building where his men were gathered, nearly hitting one of them in process. His right arm hung in a makeshift sling made from a torn blanket, which made steering awkward. The weller's shot had turned his shoulder into hamburger. Once he got a hold of the little redheaded bastard, he was going to do the same thing to the prick's head.

He brought the Crown Vic to a stop and struggled to put it into park with his left hand. He stepped out and approached the Jeep, which the men were already stripping of anything valuable. Powder stood apart from the rest, fervently rubbing his nose and sniffling.

"Where is he?"

Powder sniffed and pointed at the building. "I seen 'im run in there. He was underneath the Jeep with tools - must've been trying to get it running."

The leader looked down at the puddle of oil. The men were trampling through it, leaving black footprints everywhere. The air was thick with the smell of gasoline. This vehicle wouldn't be going anywhere - not in one piece, anyway. He stared into the inky blackness of the building. A cornered animal was the most dangerous kind, and a weller was nothing to be trifled with even under the best of circumstances.

"You in there!" the pirate leader called. "This is pointless. There's nowhere for you to run, so why don't you just come on out?"

"No thanks," came the faint reply. "Why don't you come in here?"

The pirate leader laughed. "My name's Ulrich. What's yours?"

"Nunya."

"What's that?"

"Nunya," the weller repeated. "As in, 'Nunya goddamn business.'"

Ulrich scoffed. No sense in trying to reason with the insolent little piss ant. He'd have to be dragged out, in pieces if necessary.

"Skunk! Razor!" he barked, pointing at two of the pirates looting the Jeep. "Get in there and flush that weller out!"

The two pirates turned and stared at their leader for a moment, then drew their weapons - one a crowbar and the other a length of rusty chain - and walked toward the open door. The only sounds were feet on loose sand and the whistle of the wind between the buildings. As the two pirates neared the door, their leader saw brief flashes deep in the darkness. They were small, almost indistinct, but there was no doubt about it.

They were sparks.

Suddenly the significance of the gasoline wafting in the air hit Ulrich. "Get out of there!"

The pirates froze and looked around, confused. They didn't see the sparks ignite the trail of gasoline until the flames singed their pants. The pirates watched, dumbstruck, as the fire traveled along the ground and underneath the Jeep. Ulrich dove behind his car as it reached the gas tank.

The explosion was small, but the shockwave hit the pirates like a ton of bricks, and those unfortunate enough to be standing next to the vehicle were covered in flaming gas. The oil at their feet also ignited, leaving fiery footprints all over the ground. The pirate leader stood and surveyed the damage, watching as his men rolled around and tried to extinguish the flames with their jackets and cloaks, only spreading them.

Bright lights lit up the inside of the building, and Ulrich held up a hand to shield his eyes. A loud roar erupted from the depths and reverberated off the walls. The sound of squealing tires reached his ears, and he watched as the lights came closer until a car, the most beautiful one he'd ever seen, rocketed into the night and passed the scrambling pirates.

The car was fast, a yellow streak in the night. It fishtailed to the right, striking one of the flaming pirates and sending him sailing through the air. The man's screams were drowned out by the engine's deafening roar. The car's horn pierced the night with a resounding *"Beep beep!"* Then, as suddenly as it had appeared, it was gone.

Ulrich shouted at his men, "You stupid fucks! He's getting away! After him!"

Those who were not on fire ran feebly for their vehicles, and the air was filled with the roar and whine of a dozen neglected and abused engines.

*****

Matt watched the rearview mirror and laughed as the pirates scrambled to put out the flames. The makeshift bomb had actually worked; he hadn't been sure that it would. He whipped the wheel to the right. The Road Runner turned down a side street, rocketing between the buildings at breakneck speed, peppering them with sand and gravel. Matt reached the end of the block and turned down another, reducing his speed slightly.

He looked to the left, then to the right, and he cursed. There had to be another way out of this place. The pirates had blocked the way he'd come, so the only choice was to find an alternative escape route. A glint in the rearview mirror caught his eye, and he looked up. The pirates had recovered and were chasing him.

The Road Runner came to a circle at the center of the complex, and Matt whipped the car around it, coming to a stop in front of the oncoming pirates. He revved the engine three times and took his foot off the brake, sending the car straight into a collision course with the pirate vehicles. The tires smoked and left dual lines of burning rubber as the Road Runner screamed down the street.

Matt tightened his grip on the wheel and aimed straight for the lead vehicle's headlights. With only three car lengths between him and his opponent, he honked the horn.

*Beep beep!*

This final act was all it took to send the pirate into a panic, and he wrenched his wheel to the right, sending the car off the road and through the wall of a dilapidated log cabin. Matt drove past him without so much as a glance and put his foot to the floor. The Road Runner roared like the voice of God and barreled toward the next car, a dune buggy. The driver, unwilling to take a chance in a game of chicken against the heavier Plymouth, jerked his wheel to the left to avoid the imminent collision.

The buggy's bald tires slid on the loose sand, and it flipped, striking the road on its top once before overturning into the air. Matt gunned the engine, and the Road Runner slipped under the tumbling dune buggy before it crashed back down to the asphalt. Sparks danced in the rearview mirror. Matt smiled as he turned the corner toward freedom, but his foot slammed down on the brake as he saw the Crown Vic, along with three others, at the end of the street blocking his escape route.

Ulrich sneered and lifted a .357 Magnum in his left hand, training it on the Road Runner's windshield. Matt threw the transmission into reverse as the weapon's barrel belched fire. The shot went wide, missing the Road Runner's windshield by nearly a foot. With his injured arm, Ulrich couldn't hit the broad side of a barn at this distance.

Matt stomped on the gas pedal and stuck his left hand out the window, giving the incensed pirate the finger while the Road Runner retreated.

Ulrich howled with rage and struck one of the pirates in the face with the butt of his gun. "Get him!" he bellowed over the engine's roar. "Come back with his head or don't come back at all!"

Matt wrenched on the wheel and pulled the emergency brake, letting the sand and the car's momentum whip him around. He shifted into drive, heading back the way he'd come. As he came to the twisted wreck of the dune buggy, he could see the driver feebly pulling himself free. The pirate, only dimly aware of the Road Runner barreling toward him, had gotten to his knees when the car's driver-side mirror slammed into his face at fifty miles-per-hour, killing him instantly.

Matt came once again to the circle at the center of the park and looked around desperately for any means of escape. He brought the Road Runner to a stop as his eyes rested on a massive steam locomotive to the side of the road. Two of the pirate vehicles rounded the corner, both skidding to a halt as they spotted the Road Runner. Matt looked from the pirates to the locomotive and had an idea. He frantically fought with the gear shifter, rocking the Plymouth back and forth - his left hand, concealed behind the door, held the Well Digger.

One of the pirates leaned out of his vehicle, a rusted out Chevrolet pickup truck, and shouted, "Having a little car trouble, Weller?"

The pirates laughed. While their guard was down, Matt thrust his left arm out the window and fired the Well Digger at the driver of the pickup, hitting him in the throat. The pirate, and his head, hung limp down the side of his vehicle, drenching the sandy pavement with blood spurting from his ruined carotid artery. The other pirate panicked and threw his own car, a green Nova, into gear, aiming for the side of the Road Runner.

Matt resumed his charade of fighting with the transmission until the Nova got too close to stop, then threw it into drive and stepped on the gas. The Road Runner peeled out of the Nova's path, putting the pirate on a collision course with the locomotive. Matt could barely hear his screams before the Nova slammed into the unyielding steam engine, folding the Chevy like an accordion.

Matt looked ahead and saw the visitors' center, the same building where he'd found the keys to the Road Runner, and noticed an overhead sliding door set into the side large enough to let a big rig through. He put the Road Runner into park and stepped out. The visitors' center might not offer an escape route, but it might at least buy him some time until he could take the pirates out one by one.

As he approached the door, the side of the building was illuminated behind him, casting his silhouette on the wall. He turned and saw another pirate vehicle nearing. He couldn't let the driver see him enter the building or the entire exercise would be an act of futility. As the vehicle surged toward him, he shielded his eyes with his right hand and leveled the Well Digger at the headlights with his left.

The gun roared, but the round sailed harmlessly over the car. Matt tried again, aiming lower, and this time he heard breaking glass over the roar of the engine, but the vehicle kept coming. The shriek of its fan belt pierced the night like a banshee's cry, and he knew it was too close to risk taking another shot at the driver. At the last second, he dove out of the way, and the pirate blew right past him, punching a large hole in the door and ripping it from its mechanism.

Matt covered his head as the pirate car tore into the building and crashed into the various brightly painted farm implements displayed within. When the only sound was the feeble chugging of the engine and the aggravated squealing of the fan belt, he stood and walked toward it. As his boots thumped on the fallen door, he drew the machete strapped to his thigh and raised it, ready to strike should the pirate still be capable of fighting. When he found the wreckage, however, he relaxed.

The car had crashed into an auger, and the giant drill bit had broken through the windshield and plunged into the driver's stomach. The pirate was lanky and gaunt with red-rimmed eyes and red, blistered nostrils. The inside of the car was dusted with white powder from a broken plastic bag on the dash. Even in his death throes, the poor addict reached in vain for what remained.

Matt raised the machete, ready to plunge it into the pirate's chest, but stopped. Instead, he reached in through the window and snagged the broken baggie with the tip of the blade. He dropped it unceremoniously into the pirate's blood-caked hand and sheathed the machete. The pirate struggled to look up at the weller, his expression an odd mix of anguish and gratitude.

"Thank you," Powder rasped.

Matt nodded.

The inside of the visitors' center was bathed in yellow light and Matt looked up at the entrance. At the entrance to the central circle, sat the Crown Vic. His moment of compassion had cost him his clean getaway. He dashed through the door and ran for the Road Runner.

As he got in and slammed the door, the Crown Vic roared and surged forward to cut him off. He aimed the Road Runner for the opening, and it bucked as it drove over the broken remnants of the door. It narrowly missed the rear bumper of Powder's car as Matt turned down a narrow path barely wide enough to accommodate it. The Crown Vic entered the building directly behind him, crashing into farm equipment on both sides of the pathway as Ulrich struggled to steer it one-handed.

As the path came to an end, Matt pulled the e-brake, and the car fishtailed to the left, sending it down a new turn to the right. The Crown Vic crashed into an antique Allis Chalmers tractor and then struggled around the corner. Matt came to the early automobiles display, which was arranged into a horseshoe curve; at the terminating end of it was the gift shop, which had glass walls. He smiled - he'd found his way out.

He stomped down on the gas and wrenched the wheel to the left, swinging the Road Runner's ass end to the right and sling-shotting the muscle car around the horseshoe. He straightened out the wheel and aimed for the gift shop window, his knuckles clenched tight. The Road Runner crashed through the window and plowed through the racks of moth-eaten shirts, shot glasses and postcards. It then smashed through the outer window and flew over the curb into the deserted parking lot.

The car came to a lurching stop, and Matt stared off into space for a moment before letting out a whoop of triumph. He shook, and his breath came in shaking gasps as the adrenaline caught up to him. A crashing sound from inside the building caught his attention, and he turned around in his seat. Beyond the demolished gift shop, he could see the Crown Vic struggling to get around the horseshoe curve, bumping comically into Model Ts and horseless carriages.

When Matt could finally see the pirate leader's face, he leaned out the window and shouted back at his pursuer, "Hey! Thank you kindly for visiting Fort Frontier! Come back and visit us real soon, y'hear?"

The pirate shouted back something indiscernible, and Matt laughed. He turned back around in his seat and stepped on the gas, aiming the Road Runner for the open road. Its horn rang out a parting *"beep beep,"* and it disappeared in a cloud of dust. He pointed it toward Holdrege, the last place the pirate would think to look for him, and eagerly left Fort Frontier.

Matt listened to the roar of the HEMI drifting in through the open window along with the warm desert air. He settled back in his bucket seat, letting himself become lost in the comfort of the leather. For almost ten years, he'd driven with a spring poking him in the left ass cheek. He sighed contentedly and rested his elbow on the edge of the window.

A distant light glimmered in the rearview mirror, and he looked up. Apparently he'd underestimated Ulrich. No matter. Matt maintained his course and headed for the bridge where he'd lost the pirates earlier.

*****

Several minutes later, Ulrich arrived at the broken bridge. The weller was already waiting for him with the rear end of the Road Runner facing the bridge. The pirate threw the Crown Vic's transmission into park, waiting to see what this lunatic water peddler would do next. To his surprise, the weller stepped out of his car and walked to the front, standing in the glow of the headlights.

For a moment, Ulrich considered gunning it and smashing the little bastard between their bumpers, but it would be a shame to destroy that beautiful car, and he deserved something for his troubles. After a moment of weighing his options, the pirate stepped out and walked to the front of the Crown Vic, mirroring the weller's own position.

"About time you showed up," Matt said.

Ulrich ground his teeth. "You've caused me a whole heap of trouble today, weller! This'll be a day to remember."

Matt shrugged. "For me, it's just another Monday."

The pirate drew his Magnum and hefted its weight in his weak hand. If his other arm wasn't laid up, he'd have killed this little son of a bitch an hour ago. There was no way he was going to win in a shooting match with this kid; he'd have to find a way to even the odds.

"You know," he said, taking a few steps toward his opponent. "We could shoot at each other until we both run out of bullets—"

"I only need one," said Matt.

Ulrich ignored the outburst. "Or we could settle this like civilized men."

"I'm fine with settling it like desert rats." Matt drew his massive, double-barreled revolver from beneath his coat and held it at his side.

Ulrich grinned. "Come on, now. We're both warriors - men of honor. We don't need cars or guns to settle our differences."

Matt was silent.

"Unless of course you're scared," said the pirate with a sneer.

"I'm not scared."

"Good." Ulrich tossed down his weapon. "Then let's settle this like m—"

Matt raised his weapon and fired, blowing the top of Ulrich's head clean off. The pirate's body fell to the cracked, sand-strewn pavement and twitched.

"I'm not scared," Matt repeated. "I'm just *really* fucking tired."

# Nine

The grease monkey was dreaming about a woman, and another woman, and another, all in a waist-deep pool of cold, crystal clear water. They were laughing and splashing each other. The grease monkey licked his lips in his sleep as the water glistened on their bare breasts, and he was dimly aware that he tasted something funny. Something tickled the inside of his nose, and he sneezed, coating his mouth and chin with thick strings of snot.

"*Fug!*" he slurred.

He wiped at his face, smearing mucus all over. Then he noticed the smell. It was familiar. It smelled like-

He sneezed again.

The mechanic looked up and saw a figure standing above him silhouetted in the moonlight. The figure was holding an enormous revolver in his left hand and a pepper shaker in the other, which he was pouring out onto the grease monkey's snot-covered face. As he shook the drowsiness away, the identity of his nocturnal visitor slowly dawned on him.

It was the weller!

"Evenin', friend," Matt said.

The grease monkey slowly raised his hands and tried to sit up, but Matt's steel-plated boot came down on his chest, putting him flat on his back again.

"What do you want, mister?" he whimpered.

Matt leaned in and held the pepper shaker up to his prisoner's face. "A full refund."

"What?"

"Your patch. It didn't hold. It blew about fifteen miles outside of town."

"Oh," the grease monkey mumbled. "Well, maybe I can rustle up a radiator—"

"What about my Jeep?"

"P-pardon?"

Matt crushed the pepper shaker in his fist and threw the pieces in the mechanic's face, "My Jeep! Right before your bullshit patch job failed, I got set on by 'bout a dozen road pirates! Between them and your bullshit, I'm shy one Jeep. So the way I see it, you owe me a refund - with interest."

"W-well," the grease monkey stammered, "I ain't got no Jeeps, mister."

Matt rolled his eyes. "I don't need a new Jeep, you idjit! I already got myself a replacement."

"Well, then, wh—"

"My water!" Matt snarled. "Where is it?"

The grease monkey pointed over Matt's shoulder. He turned and saw the jars sitting on top of a large tool chest. One of the jars was only three-quarters full, but the other was still sealed. Matt turned back to the grease monkey and nodded approvingly.

"Now, about the interest..." He placed the Well Digger against the mechanic's forehead.

The grease monkey let out a shrill cry and closed his eyes. Matt slowly squeezed the trigger.

*Click.*

The grease monkey's eyes snapped open, and warm urine soaked his pants, pooling around his ass. He gibbered and sobbed, sniffing loose snot back into his nose. Matt stood and jerked his head toward the door.

"Get out," he said. "And don't come back until you see my tail lights heading east. Hear?"

The grease monkey half-crawled, half-ran out of the garage. Matt listened as the man sobbed all the way down the street. He holstered his weapon and walked outside to retrieve the Road Runner.

*****

Matt worked well into the night. The first order of business was taking care of the Road Runner's paintjob. That bright yellow would attract every road pirate and desert rat for miles. It had to go. Matt searched the garage's cluttered storeroom until he found a case of black primer in spray cans. He worked slowly, covering every inch of yellow with black, non-reflective primer. By the time he was finished, the Road Runner not only looked beautiful - it looked absolutely menacing!

Next came the security system, which he'd removed from the Jeep. This was merely a matter of bolting posts to the frame to connect the battery cables to. Now anybody who tried to steal his new prize would lose their hand in the process.

Matt liberated as much as he could from the storeroom. Aside from the primer, he found a wealth of brake fluid, transmission fluid and coolant, but unfortunately he only found a single quart-sized bottle of motor oil underneath one of the shelves.

Once the loot was squared away, he made one final sweep of the building. He checked the office, which now served as the grease monkey's foul-smelling bedroom. He was about to leave when he saw an old Delco tape deck sitting on a warped wooden shelf. He picked up the radio and turned it over in his hands, inspecting the wires protruding from the back.

The shelf was also littered with small, dust-covered plastic cases. Matt picked these up and wiped the dirt from them, reading the names on the labels aloud.

"Judas Priest," he mumbled, flipping through the cases. "Metallica. ZZ Top. Black Sabbath. The Rolling Stones. Blue Öyster Cult. Aerosmith. Iron Maiden."

He opened the Iron Maiden case, removed the white cassette, and inspected it between his fingers. He lined it up with the opening in the front of the radio and slid it inside. It clicked in with little effort. He smiled and slipped the radio under his arm, scooping up all of the cassettes with his hands.

It didn't take too long to install the tape deck. Removing the useless 8-track player had been the tricky part, but once Matt had gotten the wiring exposed, swapping out the radios had been a breeze. When he turned the key, loud heavy metal music blasted from the Road Runner's speakers. He quickly hit the EJECT button, and the cassette popped out, replacing the blaring music with the soft static of a long-dead radio station. He twisted the dials until the radio finally clicked off, plunging the garage into an eerie silence.

For a moment he sat, stunned. He had heard a voice from the past, the same past which only hours ago he'd seen recreated with smiling mannequins behind Plexiglas windows. A piece of a world that, despite the best efforts of the dumb apes who had tried to destroy it, had survived. Matt slowly twisted the volume knob, bringing the volume down to a more tolerable level and pushed the cassette back into the player. He sat for several minutes, listening to voices long silent and lost to time.

He didn't quite understand the lyrics, since he didn't know the context of the words, but that didn't stop him from enjoying the song. The title offered some of the best advice he could ever get, mirroring what his grandfather had told him many years before. *Run to the Hills*, the song was called.

"Sounds like a plan," he said as he twisted the key in the ignition, bringing the Road Runner to roaring life.

He backed the car out into the street and gunned the engine, leaving the sleepy town of Holdrege, Nebraska in a cloud of exhaust. The Road Runner roared into the desert, heading straight for Omaha - if it was still there.

# PART II
# THE LAND OF PLENTY

# Ten

*"Omaha Welcomes You!"* the tilted and battered sign exclaimed.

Matt stood behind the open door of the Road Runner and gazed up at the billboard. Beyond it lay the blackened and crumbling ruins of a once-sprawling Midwestern metropolis. He stared. He hadn't seen a nuked city in over ten years, when he'd last seen Phoenix with his grandfather.

It didn't look much different, just smaller. Where the outlying areas of Phoenix had been spared from the blast, the bombs had flattened Omaha. If he waited until sundown, would the entire landscape glow? Wisps of sand, carried by the whistling wind, floated across his view of the derelict city.

"So much for that plan," he muttered, pulling a tattered roadmap from his back pocket.

While he'd had no intention of actually stopping in Omaha, it was the obvious route for crossing the Missouri River. Now he'd have to find an alternate route into Iowa. He spread the map out on the roof of the Road Runner and traced the line of the river with his finger, looking for a close - but not too close - crossing. Finally his nail came to rest on a town to the south called Plattsmouth.

The route was meandering, and there were plenty of small towns along the way, but he didn't dare risk venturing into those hamlets for fear of what kind of slow death might be awaiting him. No, better to get into Iowa and leave this radioactive hellhole far behind, he decided. He folded the map and returned it to his pocket as the wind picked up.

Behind him, he heard the sound of cracking wood and creaking metal. A gust of wind ripped the "Omaha Welcomes You!" off one of its support poles and the sign swung around, revealing the other side.

"You are now leaving Omaha. Come back soon!"

"Hmph," Matt scoffed as he entered the car and pulled the door shut behind him. "Not likely."

The Road Runner's engine came to life with a rumble and the muscle car swung south, heading for Plattsmouth - Matt Freeborn's ticket out of the nightmare that was Nebraska.

*****

It took him under an hour to cross into Iowa by way of U.S. Route 34. The landscape was thankfully less flat than its neighbor to the west, though not by a whole hell of a lot. As he passed the turnoff to Glenwood, which was a little too close to Omaha for his liking, he looked down at the Road Runner's fuel gauge. The needle was hovering precariously over "E."

*Christ.*

The old Plymouth ran like a red-tailed ape, but it sucked gas like a baby with a bottle. If he didn't find some gasoline soon, he would be stranded in the wastes with his shiny new toy collecting dust. He pulled the map out and quickly consulted it, only taking his eyes off the road for a moment. There was an intersection only a few miles ahead.

# Eleven

Matt squinted through the coat of dust clinging to his goggles at the battered road sign ahead. It was faded green and read, "MALVERN - 2 miles." He consulted the back-folded map in his dry, cracked hand.

"Population just over one thousand," he muttered, checking the map's index.

For a moment, he considered turning around and heading for Glenwood, doubting that such a puny town would have even half a gallon of usable gasoline, but a second look at the fuel gauge compelled him to reconsider.

He looked back west and frowned behind the red and white bandana covering his mouth. A dust storm was working up steam and would be upon him soon. No time to go gallivanting around the wastelands. He'd have to take his chances in Malvern.

He stepped into the car and quickly pulled the door shut, sealing him off from the howling winds. He pulled the bandana and goggles down to hang around his neck, and then scratched his dusty sideburns as he reached for the ignition. With a pump of the gas pedal and a turn of the key, the Road Runner came to life and Blue Öyster Cult's "Godzilla" blared from the speakers. Matt slammed the car into gear, and it rocketed south toward Malvern.

Since leaving Holdrege, he had listened to each one of the cassettes in his meager collection. Of all of them, Blue Öyster Cult's "On Flame with Rock and Roll" was by far his favorite. Aside from gasoline and the other usual provisions, he hoped he would be able to rustle up some new tapes while in town. Maybe he might even find more Blue Öyster Cult.

It was a long shot, but he could dream.

After about a minute, the Road Runner reached a hillcrest, and he got his first glimpse of the town, and the large pile of debris blocking the road. He cursed as he slammed his foot onto the brake pedal, mashing it against the floorboard with all of his strength. He cranked the wheel to the left at the last second, and the car skidded to a screeching halt, the rear end bumping the obstruction as it swung around. Various small odds and ends fell out of the barrier, peppering the hood and roof.

Matt stepped out of the car and took a few paces back to get a better view of the obstruction, which was a shabby - but effective - barricade made of various pieces of junk stacked approximately fifteen feet high. Washing machines, junked cars, and other useless relics of the pre-war world littered the makeshift structure. It stretched across the entire road and into the ditches on both sides, making access to the town by vehicle virtually impossible.

The barrier was obviously intended for road pirates. A fat load of good it would do, though. A heavy truck would make short work of it.

Matt looked back over his shoulder, once again considering Glenwood, but he knew that ship had sailed. He would have to take his chances on foot and hope he could make it into town before the dust storm hit. He reached inside the car to retrieve his keys and the canvas messenger bag sitting on the passenger seat, which contained three Mason jars filled with water, among other things. He'd need it if he had to trade.

He walked around to the back and opened the trunk, then removed the batteries for the Road Runner's security system. He slid underneath the car on his back and connected the jumper cables to the posts. The clamps arced when he connected them to the batteries, and the Road Runner was hot. Satisfied that his car and water were safe from bandits - at least those less sophisticated than him - he stood, pulled the bandana and goggles snug over his face, slung the bag over his shoulder, and began the long walk into town.

*****

Twenty minutes later, Matt crossed an old neglected railroad track, the rails coated in thick, red rust. As he passed underneath a crumbling concrete viaduct, he noticed white shapes poking up from behind a patch of dried up weeds. He took a few steps toward them, curious, but still anxious to get on his way. What he saw chilled the blood in his veins. The white shapes were crudely cut wooden crosses.

There didn't seem to be any order in the placement, they were simply staggered among the weeds wherever there was room. At the foot of each cross was a small pile of stones, each roughly two feet by one foot.

These were graves. Not only that, but they were *tiny* graves.

Some of the older crosses, those with their paint almost completely flaked off, bore names and dates, but the newer they were, the fewer inscriptions he saw. It was as if death had become so commonplace in this town that no one bothered with ceremony anymore. Matt adjusted his bag's shoulder strap and hurried on, trying to keep his mind off the small piles of rock.

He finally came to the edge of the town itself and walked down the dust-strewn main street. The ground felt strange under his boots - uneven - and he brushed some of the sand away. The streets were paved with bricks, not asphalt. That was definitely a new one for him.

The first thing he noticed when he began to look around was the obvious absence of human life. Normally, even in small towns like this one, people could be seen building, salvaging scrap or tending to sickly gardens, but here there was nothing moving but drifting sand. Maybe that was it - the dust storm had scared them all indoors.

Maybe.

Finally, in front of a small tavern, he saw the first signs of life. Two horses were tied to an improvised hitching post next to a watering trough. Matt approached the animals and cautiously stroked the neck of the larger - and less mangy - of the two. Obviously there were still people in this town, and now he knew where at least two of them were.

He looked down and was surprised to see the trough filled to the brim with water. Most towns in the wastelands would never allow this, even for beasts of burden, due to strict regulation. Usually, working animals were given a solution of drinking water and synthetic electrolytes developed from recycled urine. This water, however, looked strikingly clear, despite the thin skin of dust from the growing storm.

Curious, Matt reached into his pack for his testing kit, but the wind kicked up fiercely and whipped the tails of his coat around his waist. He fumbled with the buttons running down the front, trying to keep the flailing coat under control. Harsh, abrasive sand stabbed at his fingers and peppered his goggles. He looked around and saw an old service station across the street from the tavern.

"Fuel," he muttered behind the bandana.

He jogged across the street, fighting the howling wind and biting sand with every step. A dented bell jangled loudly as he opened the door and pushed back against it to lock the gale outside. He turned and saw a balding man of about fifty, thin and nearly toothless, sitting behind the counter reading a stained and wrinkled copy of *Playboy* dated January/February 2012.

"Help you?" the proprietor grunted, eyeing the weller suspiciously.

Matt didn't answer, taking a moment to remove his bandana and goggles. He shook the dust out of his hair.

"Can I help you?" said the shopkeeper, drawing out each syllable as if speaking to a foreigner, or a simpleton.

Matt stepped up to the counter. "God, I hope so. Do you have any gasoline?"

The shopkeeper looked Matt up and down with an obvious expression of dislike and distrust. "'Bout fifteen gallons."

"Is it good?"

"'Spect so," the old timer replied. "'Finers came through here about four months back."

Matt nodded. The downside to scavenging for fuel this far out in the wastes was the limited shelf life of gasoline, which would eventually evaporate, leaving behind a thick, useless sludge. Depending on storage conditions, gasoline might last as little as a couple months or as long as a couple years.

The refiners – also known as "gasmen" in other parts of the wastes - had resurrected the lost art of oil refining and sent men out to trade fuel for provisions. Pirates didn't bother them because even they knew better than to bite the hand that feeds them, but that didn't stop them from nipping at a finger every now and again - namely wellers. Besides, most 'finers packed enough firepower that any attempted robbery would be over quicker than a knife fight in a phone booth.

"How'd they get past the barricade?" Matt asked.

The shopkeeper scoffed, "Same way you did, I 'spect."

"Fair enough. I'll take ten gallons."

The shopkeeper picked up two five-gallon cans from behind the counter. "That'll be one-hundred-fifty—"

Matt cut the old man off by setting two Mason jars filled with water on the counter. "This ought to cover it."

The shopkeeper froze and stared at the water. He frowned and put away the fuel. "I don't think so. Get out."

"Wait." Matt rummaged in his pack. "That's not all. I also have batteries, ammunition, and Army rations if your inter—"

"I said get out."

"I'm sorry?" Matt couldn't believe his ears. "I don't understand. What's the problem?"

"Cash or gold, stranger." The shopkeeper returned to his magazine. "Your *water* ain't no good here."

"Bullshit! Everybody trades for water."

"You hard of hearing, outlander?" The shopkeeper stood and raised his hand, ready to swipe the offending jars off the counter. "Take your damned water and get the hell out of—"

Matt ripped open his coat, the metal snaps popping like firecrackers, and his left hand shot inside. In a flash, he drew the Well Digger and aimed it right between the shopkeeper's eyes. With

71

a flick of his thumb, he disengaged the safety, arming both cavernous barrels. The shopkeeper's eyes crossed as he stared at the gargantuan weapon.

"Touch those jars, old-timer, and I'll turn your head into a soup bowl," said Matt, cocking back the hammer for emphasis. "*Comprende?*"

The shopkeeper slowly raised his hands above his head. "Get the hell out of my place." His voice shook, shattering the illusion of his bravado.

"With pleasure, you crazy buzzard." Matt twirled the pistol backward on his finger and dropped it into the leather holster on his hip.

He collected his jars and turned toward the door, seeing the swirling dust storm through the dirty window. He looked over his shoulder. "There an inn in this town?"

"Down the street, but he don't take no water, neither."

"I'm sure I'll think of something." Matt pulled his goggles and bandana back over his face.

The ringing bell, howling wind and slamming door punctuated his departure. The shopkeeper stepped around the counter and watched as the outlander walked down the street, fighting against the abrasive winds.

*****

The sign looming over the dilapidated motel read "Color TV in every room! Free HBO!" Matt smirked behind his bandana. Having these things probably would have been a marvel for this town even before the war destroyed everything.

He stepped into the office, forced the door shut against the gale-force winds and repeated the ritual of removing the dust from his clothing. The innkeeper, a scruffy-looking blond man with a skeletal physique, sat behind the counter with his feet up. His fingers clasped a tattered paperback copy of Robert Heinlein's *The Green Hills of Earth*.

Matt approached the counter, but the man remained immersed in his book, determined not to be roused from the fantasy of spaceships, alien landscapes, and the long-gone green hills of Earth.

72

Matt cleared his throat, but this also had no effect. His eyes came to rest on a bell sitting on the counter next to the yellowed guest registry. He rang it.

The innkeeper offered him only the briefest of glances, and then returned to his reading, his lips silently mouthing the words as his eyes followed the lines on the page. Already sick of Malvern's brand of hospitality, Matt repeatedly slapped his palm against the bell, filling the room with a piercing cacophony of chimes. The innkeeper laid down his book and slapped a bony hand over the bell to silence it.

"Help you?" the innkeeper rasped.

"You got a room?"

"You got cash?"

"No."

"Then I ain't got no rooms." The innkeeper returned to his book.

Expecting such an answer this time, Matt produced a leather pouch from his pack and tossed it onto the counter. It thumped heavily on the chipped Formica. The innkeeper looked at the bag, then shifted his eyes to the weller.

Matt nodded toward the pouch.

The innkeeper dog-eared his page and tossed the paperback aside. He sat up and untied the drawstrings, then dumped the contents onto the counter. Several gold timepieces of various shapes and sizes spilled out. The innkeeper's eyes grew wide as saucers as he eagerly picked up the shiniest piece in the pile, a brilliant gold pocket watch with silver accents, and held it up to the light.

Matt grunted. *Incredible.* Normally the only people who traded for gold were dentists, who were few and far between - hell, they were damn near non-existent. To the average person, gold was about as worthless as a back pocket on a shirt, but the innkeeper seemed absolutely enamored with it.

"How long would you like the room for?" asked the innkeeper, his eyes locked on the watch.

"Just the night." Matt returned the empty pouch to his pack. "Will that be enough?"

The innkeeper nodded, his eyes still fixed on the watch between his fingers, and slid the open, dust-coated guestbook across the counter. "Oh, most certainly. Will you be needing anything else during your stay, sir? Drugs? Liquor? Women?"

"No." Matt scrawled his name in the registry, then paused and looked up. "Wait. You said liquor?"

"Yes, sir."

"Some whiskey, then." Matt put down the pen. "If you've got it."

"I do, sir. I have an entire case of it in the back. Pre-war. The *good stuff.*"

Matt paused. "A *case?* What the hell's wrong with it?"

"What?" The innkeeper blinked. "Oh, nothing. I don't indulge in it myself. It just doesn't do to get hooked on the stuff. Great for trading, though."

The weller nodded.

The innkeeper turned the guestbook around to read the outlander's entry. "Matt Freeborn. What kind of name is Freeborn?"

"It's mine."

Matt's grandfather had told him that the name was Irish, and their ancestors had come to this continent from an island called Ireland, where the hills were green, the water was clear, and the girls were pretty. He had laughed. It sounded a lot like Camelot, Disneyland, and every other bullshit fairytale land his grandparents had told him about.

Matt held out his hand. "Key?"

"Oh, yes." The innkeeper grabbed the first key on the rack. "You'll be in 1A, Mr. Freeborn - the honeymoon suite." He chuckled at his own joke.

Matt simply glared, his expression a stony mask of annoyance.

The innkeeper cleared his throat, "Will there be anything else?"

"My whiskey."

"Oh, yes!" The innkeeper disappeared into the back and returned holding a dusty - but sealed - bottle of Jack Daniel's. The bottle barely touched the counter before Matt snatched it up and turned to leave. He slammed the door shut behind him, leaving the innkeeper alone with his gold.

*****

One by one, the innkeeper pawed and fondled the shiny timepieces as if they were more precious to him than the very blood in his veins. He turned them over in his quivering fingers, noting the times on their unmoving hands. Moments frozen in time. He twisted the knob on the gold and silver pocket watch, and a quiet *tic-tic-tic-tic* filled the air. A grin spread across his face.

The door opened again, the sound startling the innkeeper back into reality. He hastily gathered up the watches and stashed them under the counter. He relaxed a bit when he saw his friend, the owner of the service station down the street, standing in the doorway. A hood and stained painter's mask protected the man from the vicious storm.

The innkeeper nodded. "Kale."

"John," said Kale, pulling off his mask and hood. "Did an outlander come in here just now?"

"Yeah, he's in room 1A. Why?"

"Did he *pay* for the room?"

"*Of course* he paid for the room! I don't give out no charity to drifters. Don't insult me."

Kale eyed his friend suspiciously. "What did he pay you *with?*"

John grinned, showing a mouthful of blackened teeth as he proudly dumped the pile of watches onto the counter. He beamed with pride, like a cat that just caught a baby bird. Kale slammed his fist onto the counter and cursed. The innkeeper's smile vanished.

"That dirty crook! He was holdin' out on me."

"What do you mean?" John wrapped a protective arm around his treasure. "Held out on you how?"

"He tried payin' me for ten gallons of gasoline with water. And all the while he had *gold*. Bastard tried to swindle me."

"Water?" John cocked his head to the side. "Why?"

Kale leaned in close and snarled, "Because he's a stinkin' *weller*, John."

John yelped, "A weller?"

Kale slapped a hand over his friend's mouth. "Quiet, you idiot. He could hear you. The walls in this hole are as thin as paper."

"What's a weller doing in Malvern? We don't need any water."

"Ain't it obvious? He wants *our* water."

"No!"

Kale nodded. "Yep. These wellers, they go from town to town looking for clean water. They don't care who they steal it from, so long as they fill their jars to peddle out in the wastes. He's come to kill us all and take our water."

"It's ours." John's eyes were full of anger and fear. "I-it's *our* water. Let them poor bastards out in the wastes find their own damned water!"

"That's right," said Kale.

"So, we gonna run him outta town, Kale?"

"No, that's no good. He'll just be back with friends."

"Then what?"

Kale pulled a shotgun from beneath his coat. "We're gonna kill 'im."

# Twelve

Matt sat alone in his room, the only illumination coming from thin pinpricks of moonlight slicing through the heavy, moth-eaten curtains onto the threadbare carpet. The howling winds propelling the dust storm across the wasteland had finally subsided, reduced now to only the occasional whistling, window-rattling gust.

Matt sat transfixed on a broken Zenith television set that lay on its side in a corner. He gazed into the spider-web fractures in the screen, allowing his brain to shut off for the first time in days. Finally, he tore himself away from the glass and took in his surroundings. The sloppily made beds were covered with filthy, stained floral comforters. Not wanting to take his chances with the unidentifiable yellow splotch on the chair, he had elected to sit on the floor against the wall directly across from the outside door.

The bottle of whiskey hung precariously from his loosely clenched fingers until suddenly his grip tightened and he lifted the bottle to his lips, taking two long pulls before lowering it again. A small stream of booze trickled down his chin, and his tongue snaked out to catch it before it could drip to the carpet, a reflex action born from many years of making every drop of moisture count. He turned the bottle over in his hands and stared at the label, so neat and... safe. Yeah, that was the word.

The last time he had found real, honest-to-God whiskey had been in a Wyoming brothel two years before. That time, the liquor had cost him a gallon of water, but damn was it worth every drop. Usually all you could find in the wastelands was moonshine. Most of it tasted only slightly better than turpentine laced with warm goat piss. Wastelanders made shine out of some of the damnedest things. He had tried carrot whiskey once in Montana; the shit had damn near killed him.

He sighed and took a long pull, swallowing twice before lowering the bottle. The innkeeper had been right about one thing - it wasn't a smart move to get hooked on anything living out in the wastes. That sorry bastard in Minden was a prime example of that - the Reaper tugging at his sleeve and the damn fool was still looking for one last fix.

Pathetic.

Well, Matt had no intention of getting hooked. A weller needed a clean head and quick reflexes, and hooch gave a man neither. For tonight, however, he had a fever, and the only prescription was more of Jack Daniel's Old Number 7.

He *could* get more, though.

There was a bag full of rings in the trunk of the Road Runner. He could clean the old man out and even have enough left over to pay off that fool with the gasoline. Hell, if these rubes wanted to trade their goods for worthless trinkets, who was he to argue? Gold was worthless, but whiskey had some weight on the bargaining table, and then of course there was the "medicinal" value.

Matt chuckled and took another swig. As he pulled the bottle away from his lips, he heard a noise – the sound of boots scraping on a sand-covered sidewalk. He placed the half-empty bottle on the carpet and groped at the floor for the Well Digger. He shook his head to ward off the spider webs clouding his vision and leveled the weapon's sight at the door. He blinked, trying to clear the double vision.

The shadows of two pairs of legs showed in the dim light filtering under the door. Matt struggled to hold the heavy weapon steady as one of the figures slipped a key into the lock.

The innkeeper.

"*Sumbitch*," he slurred. "He's after th' rest of muh damn gold."

Slowly, the knob turned, and the door opened with hesitant jerks. The hinges creaked, despite the intruder's best efforts. Matt squinted at the silhouettes framed in the doorway and tensed as the one on the left raised a shotgun.

"*Dunmove!*"

The shopkeeper laughed. "Look'it you. You're so plastered, you can barely *hold* that cannon, let alone fire it. You can't even see where you're aiming."

"With a gun this big," said Matt, "I don't need to."

The shopkeeper sighted down the shotgun's barrel at Matt's head, but before he could pull the trigger, the night exploded with the Well Digger's deafening roar. The would-be assassin gasped as the bullet tore an enormous hole in his stomach. He coughed, and blood trickled down his chin. The Well Digger fired again, and the second round struck him above the left eye, turning the left side of his head into a red, wet mist.

The innkeeper, covered in his friend's blood, screamed and turned to run away.

"Stop!" Matt shouted.

The innkeeper stopped dead in his tracks.

Matt stood, holding onto the wall with his right hand for balance, his gun arm trained carefully on the remaining intruder. His head throbbed from the thunderous discharge, his gun arm shook, and his legs were rubbery from both sitting and the drink. He staggered across the room to his sniveling, treacherous host. The innkeeper tensed and sobbed as the hot, smoking barrels of the Well Digger pressed against the back of his head.

"You stupid hick," Matt hissed. "I was gonna give you more gold in the morning for the rest of that whiskey. But you just couldn't wait, could you? You just had to have it all, didn't you?"

"We didn't want your gold," the innkeeper sobbed. "We was just protecting our water."

Matt stared at the man as if he'd sprouted a third eyeball from the back of his skull. "Your *water*?"

ADAM J. WHITLATCH

"Uh huh. Kale said you wellers get your water by stealing it from folks like us."

"*Some* wellers, maybe." Matt drove the gun barrel harder against the man's skull. "But *not me!*"

"We didn't know," sobbed the innkeeper. "But, w-we gots plenty. Take as much as you want. Jus' don't hurt me, please. I'm sorry. Take as much as you want."

"*Plenty?* As much as I want?"

The innkeeper nodded.

Matt switched the Well Digger to his right hand and reached out with his left to turn on the faucet in the washbasin beside him. The knob barely completed a full turn before a strong stream of cold, clear water spurted forth from the spigot. Matt stared, horrified, as the pressure remained constant and the clogged sink began to fill.

Instant sobriety. Just add water.

"Where does this water come from?" he asked without taking his eyes off it.

"The town reservoir," said the innkeeper.

"Show me. Now."

80

# Thirteen

The Well Digger's shots woke half the town, and the rest were awakened by the resulting commotion. Now Matt found himself, half-drunk and bleary-eyed, leading a procession of townspeople to the reservoir with the Well Digger pressed into the innkeeper's back.

Finally, the innkeeper stopped at the edge of a long-forgotten, overgrown golf course and pointed to a manhole cover set into the ground, covered in dried mud and sand. Matt looked down and shook his head.

A service reservoir.

*Christ.*

He'd gone down into plenty of these pits over the years, and most of them were just that – pits. But others were large, expansive caverns where only-god-knows-what dwelled. One time, in Colorado, he'd encountered a tribe of albino cannibals living inside one of these labyrinths. Those freaks could hardly be considered human anymore; time and perpetual darkness had reshaped them into something much more primeval.

Matt shuddered at the prospect of what might await him below. He'd give about anything for another swig of that whiskey right about now.

He motioned toward the manhole with the Well Digger. "Pry it up."

The handle of a discarded golf club served as a crude pry bar, and the innkeeper chipped away at the mud until he could get the tool into the grooves along the edge. Matt kept his eyes on the innkeeper, but his ears were focused on the townspeople gathered around him. Some of them were merely curious, but others had much more murderous thoughts.

The innkeeper lifted the lid and slid it aside with a strained groan. A whistling, underground breeze echoed from the hole. So much for any hope that the reservoir was sealed.

"Down," said Matt

"W-what?"

Matt placed the gun under the innkeeper's chin. "You think I'm stupid enough to go into that hole first? Down. Now."

The innkeeper nodded and descended the rusty iron ladder, disappearing into the depths. Matt holstered the Well Digger and followed. As he descended, he noticed a smell that got stronger the farther down he traveled. It was unlike anything he'd ever smelled, but it was unquestionably animal. Something was definitely living down here, but he'd expected that.

When his boots finally touched solid ground, he heard the innkeeper's voice calling out meekly from the shadows. Matt cracked a glow stick from his pack and shook it vigorously, filling the chamber with an eerie green light.

The innkeeper, attracted by the light, quickly ran to the weller's side. As he walked, Matt could hear and feel small bones crunching under his boots. Less than ten yards from the ladder, the ground gave way to an immense lake of shimmering water. Brick pillars and arches supported the ceiling.

"Y'see?" said the innkeeper. "I told you we got plenty. Take as much as you want."

"Shut up," Matt snapped. "And don't touch anything."

He knelt and began digging through his bag, the glow stick clenched between his teeth. At the bottom, he found what he was looking for: the Geiger counter.

He switched on the machine, and a furious clicking sound echoed through the chamber. As he waved the wand over the lake, the chattering morphed into a continuous burst of static.

"Jesus hopped-up Christ," Matt whispered around the glow stick in his mouth.

"What does it say?" asked the innkeeper.

Matt stood and removed the glow stick. "This water's so goddamned radioactive you people should glow in the fucking dark."

"But nobody's sick!" the innkeeper protested.

Matt nodded, pondering the innkeeper's observation. It was true, nobody he'd encountered seemed to be sick. A little thin and scurvied maybe, but nothing - then he remembered something.

"The graves."

"What?"

"The children. I haven't seen a single child since I came into town. Where are they?"

The innkeeper suddenly looked very uncomfortable. "Gosh, there ain't been a child born in this town since..."

He didn't need to say it. Matt already knew the answer.

*Since the war.*

"What should we do?" asked the innkeeper.

"Do?" Matt shoved the Geiger counter into his bag and carefully made his way back to the ladder; no sense in bothering with chemical tests. "Get yourself a damned good weller."

A loud hissing sound emanated from the shadows behind them.

The innkeeper jumped. "What was that?"

Matt squinted, and his heart jumped as several pairs of eyes blinked at him from out of the darkness, the glow stick giving them an ominous green glow.

He drew the Well Digger. "Trouble."

One by one, several large, furry bodies with pale, hairless tails slinked into the light. The animals were roughly the size of coyotes and covered in gray and white hair. The closest of the critters hissed at the humans, displaying a maw full of sharp, white teeth.

"Great," said Matt. "Radioactive water *and* giant mutant rats. This place gets better and better."

"They're not rats," said the innkeeper, a look of horror on his face. "They're 'possums!'"

"'Possums?" Matt risked a bewildered glance at the innkeeper. "You've got to be fucking kidding me!"

The lead opossum lunged and Matt opened fire; the weapon's deafening roar reverberated through the entire cavern. The animal exploded in a spray of blood and viscera. Those that didn't stop to feed on their fallen leader advanced on the humans. Matt fired three more times in quick succession, but the mutant marsupials kept coming. He opened the breach of the massive pistol with a flick of the wrist and held the weapon out to the innkeeper.

"Reload."

"W-what?"

Matt fished a handful of cartridges from his coat pocket and dumped them into the innkeeper's outstretched hand. "Hurry!"

While the innkeeper fumbled with the massive weapon, Matt drew the machete strapped to his leg and slashed at an approaching mutant. Its severed head rolled into the lake and bobbed like a cork.

"Ugh." Matt grimaced. "I'd seriously stop drinking that water now if I were you."

One opossum leaped at him, and he kicked it out of the air. The steel-plated toe of his boot connected with the beast's face and cracked its teeth. Another mutant came too close, and Matt sliced through the corners of its open mouth with the machete.

The innkeeper finally slid the sixth shell home and handed the gun back to the weller. Matt switched the machete to his right hand and covered the hissing mutants with the Well Digger in his left.

"Climb," he said, training the gun on the nearest mutant.

"What about you?"

"I'll be right behind you. Now go!"

The innkeeper climbed frantically, putting as much distance between himself and the hissing monsters as possible. Satisfied that the mutants weren't going to rush him again, Matt sheathed the machete and ascended the ladder.

The inquisitive chattering of the townspeople grew louder with every rung he climbed, but it was another sound that drew his

84

attention - the sound of hissing at his feet. He looked down and saw one of the opossums scaling the ladder behind him, nipping at his heels. He lowered the Well Digger, clicked off the safety and fired both barrels simultaneously, effectively vaporizing the mutant's head and upper body, but its thick, bald tail continued to cling to the ladder even in death.

Matt pulled himself out of the cold, clammy atmosphere of the reservoir and into the warm, dry Iowa air. He holstered the pistol and helped the innkeeper drag the manhole cover back into place. It clanked home, silencing the rising hisses from within. Over a hundred townspeople converged upon the shaken men, and again Matt couldn't help but notice that there was not a single child among them.

Countless cries overlapped each other as the townspeople attempted to quench their thirst for gossip.

"What's wrong?"

"Is something wrong with our water?"

"What's happening?"

"What's down there?"

This was undoubtedly the most excitement the town had seen since the bomb had dropped on Omaha, and now Matt was about to drop another one.

"Everybody, settle down!" he shouted, struggling to be heard.

But the crowd was either unable or unwilling to give him their full attention, and continued to question both him and the innkeeper about the events unfolding beneath their town. Losing his patience, and feeling the beginnings of a massive headache, Matt raised the Well Digger above his head and fired. The pistol's report echoed, bouncing back off the dilapidated buildings. Immediately, the crowd grew silent, and every eye in Malvern was focused on him.

"Listen up," he said. "Your reservoir has been contaminated by radiation. The water is no longer safe to drink."

"Bullshit!" called a male voice from the back.

A plump, middle-aged woman in a patched pink dress called out to him, "What can we do? Is there any way to clean the water?"

Matt shook his head. "It's too far gone. But you've got even bigger problems. The radiation has mutated the animals living inside the reservoir and has made them aggressive. Your best option is to just evacuate the town and relocate to a new settlement before they find their way up to the surface. I do have some water with me that can help get the town started on the journey, but it's not much. I trade for fuel, batteries, and food - but, please, no food that has been cooked or grown with this water. Oh, and, uh... music cassettes, if you've got 'em."

"How do we know you're telling the truth?" yelled a man from the back of the crowd.

Matt pointed at the manhole cover. "Why don't you stick your head in that hole and find out for yourself? Here's another question for you: When was the last child born in this town? I'm willing to bet not since the war. Am I right? Close?"

"Go to hell!" shouted the woman in the pink dress.

This sentiment was obviously shared by the rest of the townspeople as the others began to yell, spit, and throw rocks at Matt. He ducked one of the larger stones and came back up with the Well Digger clasped in his left hand. Slowly, he sidestepped around the edge of the crowd, never turning his back on them. Hate-filled, paranoid eyes met his steely gaze.

As he finally reached the back of the crowd, placing himself between them and the town, a man in a battered straw hat cried out, "Go home, outlander! Go hawk your piss-water out in the wastes."

A woman behind him yelled, "Ain't nothin' wrong with our water. You're just trying to cheat us!"

"No," said the innkeeper. "He's tellin' the truth. There really are creatures down there!"

"Shut up, John," said one of the older men. "Can't you see he's trying to trick us into leaving so he can steal our water?"

"We'll see." Matt walked backwards toward town, keeping the mob covered with the gun. "We'll see."

A loud metallic thumping sound rang out behind the townspeople, and the women shrieked, startled by the suddenness of the sound. Matt forced his way through the crowd for a better look.

The manhole cover shook and rattled.

"Damn," Matt breathed.

As the metal disc slowly rose and fell with the exertion of the animal below, Matt began reloading his weapon. As he closed the breach, as if on cue, the manhole cover was flipped aside, and one of the mutants sprang from the hole, hissing at the frightened mob.

"Holy shit," someone yelled. "He was telling the truth!"

Matt cocked the Well Digger and aimed at the mutant. "O ye of little faith."

He squeezed the trigger, and the opossum's head exploded, spraying the onlookers with blood and brain matter. He turned and shouted at the crowd, "Everybody get ba—"

Something heavy and warm struck him on the back and forced him to the ground, knocking the wind out of him. He struggled against the weight, and when he saw the thin string of saliva dripping past his face and felt the hot breath on his ear, he realized the gravity of his predicament. He rolled onto his back and over the mutant, coming to rest a few feet away from the bloodthirsty marsupial. He jerked the machete from its sheath and brought it down on the creature's spine, severing it. The opossum shrieked and clawed at the earth while its back half lay limp and lifeless.

Matt got to his feet and took in the chaos unfolding around him. Everywhere he looked, mutants were attacking the townsfolk. Nearby, he saw one of the freaks pinning down the woman in the pink dress, tearing large hunks of flesh from her plump legs with its teeth. He ran toward them and kicked the mutant in the jaw, sending it tumbling away.

Matt knelt to pick up the woman, but she was in hysterics, slapping and scratching at him. He punched her in the face, and her eyes rolled back. He grabbed her unconscious body by the shoulders and tried to drag her to safety. They made it twelve feet before the opossum that had been attacking her leaped and clamped down tight on her throat, spraying its whitish-gray fur with the woman's blood.

Matt fired a quick shot at the mutant, blowing away a sizable chunk of its hindquarters. The mutant jerked and looked up at him; it bared its sharp, blood-coated teeth and screeched. Matt chambered another round, and then put it right through the mutant's gaping maw. Blood and brains exploded out the back of its skull.

Matt looked up and saw more of the mutant freaks crawling out of the reservoir, each fighting to get out before its pack mates. This was a lost cause. These things would soon overrun the town. There was only one thing he could do.

*Run, Mattie.*

The weller turned and ran toward town as fast as his legs would carry him.

# Fourteen

*I'm going to die here.*

Try as he might, Matt couldn't push the thought from his mind.

The townspeople's screams were fading behind him, the endless din broken up by the occasional gunshot. He fancied that he heard the skittering of clawed feet behind him, but saw nothing in the darkness.

He stopped for a moment to get his bearings and catch his breath; the whiskey sloshing in his gut weighed him down. He was fairly certain that following the next street left would take him back to the main street. From there, he could find his way to the service station and-

A low hiss sounded from somewhere to his right, but he couldn't spot the source in the darkness. He whirled as another hiss from behind joined the first. He raised the Well Digger, but then reconsidered and lowered the weapon. There was no telling how many of these freaks were in the town, and he didn't have enough bullets to take them all out. He needed to concentrate on escaping - and that meant he needed fuel.

He ran, leaving the unseen monsters in the shadows.

*****

The door to the service station was locked. Of course it was. There was a "dangerous outlander" in town, after all. Matt kicked the door above the knob, splintering the jamb and sending the door swinging.

It was pitch black inside the shop, so he pulled another glow stick from his pack.

Bathing the room in green light, he looked behind the counter and found the two five-gallon cans right where the shopkeeper had left them. A third lay a short distance away. For a moment, he considered devising a way to carry it, but then remembered the hissing monsters waiting for him outside. Hauling the extra can would only slow him down.

With the glow stick clenched between his teeth, he hefted the cans and stepped outside, expecting to hear hissing, but instead was greeted by the equally ominous sound of a shotgun shell being chambered. An old man brandishing a twelve-gauge stood between him and the street; blood dripped from a ragged bite in the man's forearm.

"Freeze, outlander!" the old codger shouted.

Matt rolled his eyes. *"Aww, fit!"* he mumbled around the glow stick.

"Drop the cans," the old man ordered.

Matt stared. *"Are oo fufhing hidding me?"*

The old man took a labored step forward. "You haven't done enough? Now you have to steal from us, too?"

*"I didn't do fit!"*

"Spit that out," the old man barked. "I want to hear you beg for your life before I pump you full of lead."

Matt wondered if he could drop the cans and draw the Well Digger before the old coot pulled the trigger. He was still calculating his odds when he saw a pair of reflective eyes creeping up behind his captor. He spat out the glow stick.

"Behind you!" Matt shouted.

But the old man wasn't having any of it. He leveled the shotgun, and Matt tensed, ready to try for his weapon. Just then, an opossum latched onto the man's leg, and he pulled the trigger as he was jerked to the ground. The gun went off, and Matt heard the pellets of buckshot whizzing over his head. He watched as the mutant shook its head back and forth like a dog and tore a ragged hunk of meat and cloth from the man's leg. The opossum's eyes shone in the light from the glow stick as it chewed contentedly.

Matt dropped the cans and reached into his coat, but then slowly took his hand out. Why bother? The old codger was dead anyway and, besides, would he have given Matt the same courtesy?

Hell no.

These people wouldn't piss on his head if his hair caught fire. Better to escape with his skin. Honor was a disposable commodity.

The man on the ground kicked at the feeding mutant and reached for the shotgun, which had fallen a few inches out of reach. His fingers stretched out to brush the stock, but clenched in agony as the marsupial took another bite from his calf. Matt kicked the shotgun into the man's groping hand; he could spare that much honor for him.

He picked up the cans and paused to look back at the inn down the street. There was still a good half a bottle of whiskey in his room and God only knew how much in the innkeeper's office. He could easily carry three bottles in his pack - maybe four or even five!

A single shotgun blast behind him helped him make his decision.

It was time to go.

*****

Carrying the cans and traveling in the dark slowed him down, but Matt reached the Road Runner without further incident. In his panic, he almost forgot to disable the security system. The idea of being eaten alive by those freaks with his hand fused to the side of a car made him shudder. As he stowed the batteries in the trunk, he noticed an orange glow over the horizon. Something in town was burning.

Casting constant glances over his shoulder, Matt emptied both fuel cans into the Road Runner's tank and tossed the empties into the trunk. As he slammed it, he heard the familiar hissing. He drew the Well Digger and walked toward the driver's side door, his back pressed against the car. He reached the door and breathed a sigh of relief as he shut it behind him.

A turn of the key later, the Plymouth roared to life, and Blue Öyster Cult drowned out the muffled hissing. Matt turned on the headlights and illuminated the road ahead of him, revealing half a dozen mutant opossums, their teeth bared and recoiling from the harsh glare.

He slammed the transmission into gear and threw the muscle car into a fishtailing U-turn, bashing one of the mutants against the passenger-side quarter panel. He watched the animals' glowing eyes fade into the distance in the mirror, until all he could see was the orange glow above Malvern.

The fuel gauge's needle now hovered above the 3/4 mark, which was plenty to carry him far, far away from this radioactive nuthouse. He settled back in his seat and twisted the volume knob on the radio.

The speakers blared the tale of Tokyo's destruction, and he drove on, oblivious to the parallels between the song's lyrics and his recent brush with death. The folly of man had indeed been pointed out that day.

"Go, go, Godzilla," the weller sang along.

# PART III
# KOOZY

# Fifteen

Matt pulled the skin of his cheek taut and dragged the blade of the pink Lady BIC downward. The sound of the steel against his rough, dry stubble was like sandpaper, but the sensation was a welcome one. Carefully, he ran the plastic shaver over his face, with only his sweat to lubricate it, and removed the coarse, ginger-colored hair. It left his skin smoother than he'd seen it in years. He rubbed his face and smiled at his reflection in the Road Runner's side mirror.

To get a decent shave in the wastes, one normally had to find a barber and pay through the nose. Lather tended to be quite expensive, and Matt had yet to run across a can of the stuff during his adventures.

The razors had been a rare find in an abandoned Walmart in Mount Pleasant, Iowa the night before. He'd found a pack of eight on the floor, forgotten underneath a shelf. To his surprise, only one of the razors had been broken - a good thing, too, because the rest of the night had been a total bust.

Satisfied with his shave, he tossed the BIC into the open center console between the front seats. He pulled the red and white bandana from his back pocket and wiped his face before tying it loosely around his neck. A light breeze picked up and tickled his clean skin, a rare sensation for a man of his station. As abruptly as it started, the wind ceased, and he was brought back to reality.

He lifted his duster from the Road Runner's trunk and shook it vigorously, ridding the battered and fraying cloth of about a week's worth of dust and sand. He then draped it over the roof of the car to let the wrinkles out.

His stomach growled, so loud it sounded almost like a rumbling engine. He looked to the north and south, seeing nothing but cracked asphalt in either direction all the way to the horizon.

"You've been in the sun too long," he told himself. "Look at you - you're beginning to talk to yourself."

He leaned in through the open window, pushed a black cassette into the tape deck, and twisted the volume knob hard to the right. Judas Priest's *Turbo Lover* boomed from the speakers, and he nodded his head approvingly. He opened the trunk and reached into a tattered burlap bag tucked into a corner. He felt around inside until his fingers closed around a small tin can.

He turned it over in his hands. It had no label, like most pre-war food cans. In the weeks following the battle, rodents and insects had taken over the supermarkets, tearing into the bags and boxes. When that food supply had run out, the vermin had then turned to the labels and glue on the cans, leaving the impenetrable aluminum behind for looters to ponder over. Matt lifted the can to his ear and shook it, listening to the sloshing contents.

"Could be oranges," he mused. "Could be mushrooms."

He hoped for oranges, even though he knew better than to put that much faith in chance. He pulled a Swiss Army knife from his hip pocket and flipped open the can opener, carefully moving the blade up and down along the rim of the tin. When the lid lifted, he could hardly believe his luck. Nestled inside were seven Vienna sausages.

Matt threw his head back and laughed up at the heavens. "Meat!" he cried jubilantly.

He couldn't remember the last time he'd eaten meat that he didn't have to kill first. He wasn't squeamish about killing - that was unfortunately part of his job description - but cleaning and butchering game took more time and effort than he could usually spare.

This was a real treat.

He rummaged in the trunk until he found a can of Sterno. He placed it on the ground and pried the lid open with his knife, then pulled the flint from his pocket and struck it against the blade. The sparks ignited the blue gel instantly, and a bright flame rose from the can's opening. Matt speared a sausage with his pocketknife and held it over the fire. As he cooked his breakfast, he heard a noise growing steadily over the music blaring from the car, and it wasn't his stomach.

It was engines.

This time he was sure of it.

He stood and looked north, and then south. That's when he saw it - the telltale glisten of sunlight on windshields. He watched as a single shape, soon followed by several more, rose over a hill and barreled toward him. He brought the knife up to his mouth and pulled the sausage off the blade with his teeth.

"Fuck me," he mumbled through a mouthful. "Pirates."

He blew out the Sterno and scooped it up, juggling the hot can between his hands as he struggled to replace the lid and stow it in the trunk. He slammed the trunk and ran to collect his coat. But when he turned to look at the approaching vehicles, he noticed something odd. The lead vehicle was swerving back and forth - an evasive maneuver.

The pirates were already chasing someone.

Matt tossed his coat into the back and dove in through the window to grab the Well Digger from the passenger seat, snagging his goggles from the dash as he exited the vehicle. He slipped the goggles over his eyes as a red and white 1972 GMC pickup blew past him. Nearly fifteen pirate vehicles ranging from modified station wagons to motorcycles with sidecars were closing in on the truck, the drivers whooping and hollering taunts at their prey.

"Son-of-a-*bitch*," said Matt, watching the GMC as it passed. "Radar."

The last vehicle in the pack, a modified dune buggy with an exposed engine, skidded to a halt in front of the stunned weller. Two pirates with blackened teeth, one armed with a knife and the other with a pickaxe, jumped out of the buggy and advanced on him. Matt calmly aimed the Well Digger at the pirates and sneered as their eyes widened at the sight of the colossal weapon. He thumbed the safety, and they simultaneously dropped their weapons and climbed back into the dune buggy, taking off the way they came.

Matt pulled open the door and was about to pursue them when he suddenly remembered his breakfast. He cursed, ran to retrieve the can, and reentered the car. The HEMI roared to life, and the back tires dug into the gravel a moment before propelling the Road Runner onto the cracked, uneven asphalt like a rocket.

Normally Matt would leave the pirates to their own devices, thankful that they weren't after him, but this was an extenuating circumstance. Scott "Radar" Rice, known for his excellent sense of hearing and uncanny ability to detect underground springs, was a weller. A damned good one, too. Moreover, he was one of Matt Freeborn's few living friends. Matt picked a cold sausage out of the tin nestled between his legs and popped it into his mouth.

"What's that dumb son-of-a-bitch gotten himself into this time?" he said as he chewed.

It didn't take long for Matt to overtake the rear vehicle in the pack. He nudged the station wagon's rear bumper with the Road Runner's nose. The pirate wheeled around in his seat and snarled as Matt waved at him, honking his car's signature *BEEP BEEP* horn. The station wagon's passenger climbed into the back to man the machine gun mounted to the roof.

Matt gunned the accelerator and whipped the Road Runner alongside the pirate vehicle. He aimed the Well Digger at the car's fender and fired. The bullet punched through the engine block, spraying oil and antifreeze all over the windshield. The driver panicked and lost control, veering through a guardrail and into a deep culvert.

Up ahead, the lead car in the pack, a white 1963 Thunderbird convertible, rammed into Radar's pickup, rocking it slightly onto two wheels. Matt watched as his friend reached out and aimed a sawed-off twelve-gauge shotgun at the T-bird and fired, peppering the hood but not hitting anything vital.

Matt counted three men riding in the convertible. The one in the rear, a large man wearing a black leather motorcycle jacket, was reclining with his arms stretched out over the back seat. The man slapped the shoulder of the pirate in the passenger seat and pointed at the truck.

The pirate stood, and then leaped into the bed of the pickup. Radar jerked the wheel to the right, sending the pirate tumbling around the bed, but the marauder grabbed onto the roll bar and quickly regained his footing.

Matt cursed as the pirate began tossing jerry cans of water and fuel to the large man in the back seat of the T-Bird. He tried to maneuver around a battered Pontiac GTO to reach the other weller's truck, but the driver jerked the wheel and slammed his car into the right side of the Road Runner, scraping off primer and exposing the original yellow paint beneath.

"You father-rapin' sack of shit!" Matt snarled.

He aimed the Well Digger through the open window and fired both barrels. The driver's head exploded, painting the inside of the car crimson, and the Pontiac veered off into one of the motorcycles, sending both vehicles into a ditch.

Back in the GMC, Radar was trying desperately to shake the pirate from the bed, but to no avail. Finally the pirate tossed the last jug of water to his cohorts and made his way to the front of the truck. While Radar struggled to reload his shotgun and maintain control of the truck, the pirate jerked open the passenger-side door. Matt watched, muttering as Radar tried to shove his gun into the pirate's face, but the man grabbed his wrist and yanked the shotgun away, blowing a large hole in the truck's back window.

The truck swerved violently back and forth across both lanes as the pirate and the besieged weller fought for control of the wheel. The truck's speed decreased as Radar kicked at his opponent. The T-Bird pulled up alongside the truck again, and the large, leather-clad man stood to open the door of the GMC. While the large pirate tested his footing, Matt surged past a dune buggy and rammed the T-Bird's rear bumper. The pirate stumbled and fell onto the T-Bird's trunk.

Matt's eyes locked with the pirate's for a moment; they were filled with shock and rage. The pirate stood and prepared to jump onto the Road Runner's hood. As he was about to spring, Matt stomped on the brake pedal with both feet, dropping the speed by about thirty miles-per-hour. The pirate screamed as he fell face first onto the cracked asphalt and rolled.

Matt stepped on the gas pedal, and the Road Runner surged toward the fallen pirate. The muscle car shuddered, and Matt was lifted out of his seat as the marauder was crushed under the tires. Matt calmly dug another sausage out of the tin and popped it into his mouth, not bothering to look in the rearview mirror at the mangled mess.

The truck had slowed to a near crawl, but the T-Bird was blocking any chance of a clear shot at Radar's attacker. Matt stuck the Well Digger out the window and aimed for the driver, but the shot missed, hitting the top of the passenger seat and going through the windshield. The shot caught the attention of both the driver of the T-Bird and the brawlers inside the truck. The pirate in the pickup took advantage of the distraction and pushed the driver's side door open. Radar, who had been pressed up against the door, fell out and hit the ground tumbling.

The pirate pulled the door shut and laughed triumphantly as he guided the stolen truck down the road. The other pirates ignored the fallen weller and continued down the road, their objective completed. Radar looked up in time to see the Road Runner bearing down on him and closed his eyes, waiting for the inevitable impact. Matt braked hard and jerked the wheel to the left, swinging the car around and bringing the passenger-side door right alongside Radar.

"Get in!"

Radar opened his eyes and looked inside the car, hardly believing his eyes. "Matt? Is that you?"

"Get in," Matt repeated. "We can still catch them."

Radar stood on shaky legs and folded his tall, lanky form into the leather bucket seat, and the Road Runner took off the second the door slammed shut. Matt swung the car around and punched the accelerator, intent on catching the retreating pirates.

"Why'd they throw out your cargo if they were just going to take the truck too?" Matt asked.

Radar shrugged, wincing at the pain the gesture caused his sore shoulder. "Maybe they were afraid I'd wreck the truck."

Matt nodded. "I would have."

Radar grinned. "I know you would've."

Matt squinted through the dusty windshield at the rear vehicle in the pack. "What the hell are they doing?"

Radar's eyes went wide in horror as a pirate stood up in the back of a green pickup truck, holding a red five-gallon plastic fuel can with a lit road flare taped to it. The pirate tossed the can underhanded, and it sailed through the air toward the Road Runner.

"Shit!" Radar yelled.

"Hang on!" Matt slammed on the brakes and jerked the wheel to the left.

The can struck the pavement, and the lid popped off, sending gasoline directly onto the lit flare. The fuel ignited, and the can exploded in a massive fireball a few feet away from Radar's window. Radar turned away as the intense heat singed the tips of his hair. Matt scrambled out of the car and pointed the Well Digger over the hood at the retreating pirates, but they were already out of range. Radar got out and kicked away the melting fragments of the can.

"Those pirates are fucking crazy," said Radar, rubbing the right side of his face.

Matt holstered his gun and nodded. "Crazier than most."

Radar looked down at the muscle car between them and stroked the hood reverently. "My God, Freeborn, where did you get this magnificent machine?"

"Minden," Matt said. "Nebraska. A little speck in the dirt called Fort Frontier. They've got a whole building full of cars like this, every last one of them as cherry as a preacher's daughter."

Radar grinned. "Well then who needs a truck? Let's go get me a car."

Matt shook his head. "I ain't going back to Nebraska. Not on your life! You can do that on your own time if you want."

Crestfallen, Radar hung his head and sighed.

Matt leaned over the hood. "Nebraska's a long walk. The way I see it, you're going to need that truck if you plan on getting there before the Second Coming."

Radar looked up, a grin spreading across his face. "You're going to help me get it back?"

"You think I'd just leave you wandering around the wastes alone?" Matt opened the driver's side door. "I'm *offended*. Besides, you're sure as hell not hanging around with me. 'Bout two... three days is about all I can stand of you."

Radar clutched his chest and feigned devastation. "Oh, Matthew! Don't talk like that. Don't deny our *love!*"

Matt opened his coat, revealing the Well Digger, and pointed a warning finger at his friend. "You keep up that kind of talk and I'll make sure you *crawl* to Nebraska!"

Radar grinned.

Matt sighed and looked toward the northern horizon. "Well, we're about fifteen miles from Iowa City, I'd say. It stands to reason that's probably where they're headed."

"But what if it's not?" Radar pulled a tattered roadmap out of his back pocket and smoothed it out on the hood. "Look at this. Iowa City sits right on Interstate 80."

Matt shrugged. "So?"

"So?" Radar shouted. "So from there they can go *anywhere* - east *or* west."

Matt shook his head. "I don't think so. They didn't look like nomads to me. These boys are local."

Radar stared at the map and shook his head.

Matt studied it for a moment. "Where were you when they started chasing you?"

"Around Ainsworth." Radar pointed to a spot on the map. "I was welling in a truck stop down there."

"They probably wouldn't travel more than an hour." Matt traced the road north with his finger. "Here. What about Cedar Rapids?"

Radar shook his head. "Gone."

"Nuked?"

"Glows in the goddamned dark."

Matt slapped the map with the back of his hand. "Then it's got to be Iowa City."

"And if it's not? The trail could go cold while we're chasing your wild hunches!"

Matt considered this; Radar certainly wasn't wrong. He chewed his lip. Then it came to him.

"There was a buggy."

Radar blinked. "Buggy?"

"When I first saw you, two pirates in a dune buggy tried to rob me. I flashed the Digger at them, and they tucked tail. Headed south."

"South," Radar mused. "They'll have to come back this way to hook back up with their gang."

"And when they do—"

"We tail 'em back home." Radar grinned.

Matt tapped his nose and smiled, then walked back to the driver's door.

Radar settled into the passenger seat. "Matt ol' buddy, this is gonna be just like the old days back in Arizona."

Matt shut his door and turned the key with a wry grin. "That's what scares me."

# Sixteen

"Think anyone's still up there?"

"Hmmm?" Matt grunted, his brain lingering somewhere between sleep and consciousness.

"Up there," Radar repeated, nudging Matt's shoulder.

Matt opened his eyes and blinked. Radar was pointing up at the windshield. Matt looked out the driver's side window, past the battered billboard they were parked behind, and up at the ink-black sky dotted with twinkling white stars.

"What the hell are you jawing about, Radar?"

Radar sat up in the passenger seat and twisted the volume knob on the radio, reducing Blue Öyster Cult's "Astronomy" to barely over a whisper.

"Well," Radar said, "my daddy used to tell us stories about men who lived in huge metal ships that circled the planet."

Matt grunted. His grandfather had told him similar fairytales.

"If that's true," Radar continued, "then maybe they're still up there... watchin'. Waitin' for the air and the water to clear up so they can come back down here to live. Ya think?"

"Don't be stupid, Radar."

"You don't believe in anything, do you, Matt?"

Matt reached into his coat and withdrew the Well Digger, holding it up for his companion to see. "I believe in this."

Radar held out his hand, and Matt dropped the heavy revolver into his waiting palm. Radar hefted it, marveling at how small the weapon made his hand look. This weapon was legendary; tales of its power and the devastation left in its wake followed its owner all over the wasteland. If the wastes respected anything, it was the Well Digger. And if there was anything it feared, it was the hand that wielded it.

"You miss him?" Radar whispered.

Matt sighed. "Every goddamn day."

"Your grandfather was a good man, Matt. The best of us."

"You don't have to tell me that," said Matt, taking the Well Digger back.

The wellers sat in silence, both mesmerized by the starlight reflecting off the revolver's surface. Radar laughed.

Matt shifted in his seat to get a better view of his companion. "What's so funny?"

"Remember that time we were scoping out that cistern near Hoteville?"

Matt snorted. "How can I forget? You fell in and thought you were going to drown, so you pissed your pants. Didn't matter it weren't no deeper than five feet."

"Yeah," Radar chortled. "Your gramps was so pissed, he screamed at me, 'Scottie Rice, you dust brain! I hope you're thirsty, cuz I'll be *damned* if I'm gonna drink your piss!'"

Matt laughed and wiped a tear away with one rough, calloused finger. When he opened his eyes, he saw Radar's face much clearer than before, and a glow began to fill the inside of the car. The strained sound of a small engine ripped apart the cold stillness.

They watched as the dune buggy blew past the billboard and tore over the broken asphalt, heading north.

"About damn time," said Radar. "Let's get after 'em!"

Matt nodded and waited until he was satisfied the buggy was well out of earshot, then turned the key and awakened the sleeping Road Runner. He pulled onto the highway, keeping his lights off, using the buggy's taillights as a guide - a risky tactic on unfamiliar roads, but one he had employed many times over the years. So long as the pirates kept their eyes on the road, they would be safe.

He hoped.

# Seventeen

Thirty minutes later, the dune buggy and its shadowy pursuer crested a hill. What the wellers saw on the horizon froze the blood in their veins. Lights pierced the inky blackness - not headlights or twinkling stars, but something neither man had seen in years.

City lights.

"I'll be goddamned," Radar whispered.

In the brief flash of the buggy's headlights, Matt saw a tilting green sign.

IOWA CITY - NEXT 3 EXITS

Matt sighed. "Shit. They *are* heading into the city."

Matt took his foot off the accelerator and let the Road Runner coast to a stop, watching the buggy's taillights fade into the distance.

"What're you doing?" Radar demanded.

Matt watched as the buggy took the second off-ramp and disappeared into the city, its lights mingling with the many others. It was these very lights that had Matt so rattled; it wasn't their presence - though that was unsettling enough. No, it was something about their placement. Radar's frantic wailing made it impossible for him to concentrate on the riddle.

"Shit!" Radar punched the dash. "They're getting away! Good going, you dust brain."

As the Road Runner rolled to a stop, Matt threw the transmission into "park" and turned to face his companion.

"Calm down," he said, opening his door and stepping out.

He walked to the front of the car and looked over the city. A cold wind whistled through the air and tugged at the bandana tied around his neck. He stood as silent as a statue, his coat tails whipping violently about his legs. Radar stepped out of the Road Runner and slammed the door, a sound like a gunshot in the deathly silent wasteland.

Radar stalked over to his silent friend. "You want to explain just what the hell we're doing out here? Our best lead - no, our *only* lead - just disappeared like a fart in the wind, and you're just standing there with your thumb up your ass!"

Matt's eyes narrowed, staring right over Radar's shoulder. "Calm down," he repeated.

Radar balled up his fist and took a clumsy swing at his friend. "Don't tell me to calm down, you son-of-a-bit—"

Matt sidestepped the punch and grabbed Radar's wrist with his right hand, then pushed on his shoulder and slammed the angry weller face-first into the hood of the car.

"Calm *down*," Matt repeated, this time with much more urgency. "I didn't lose them, Radar. I know exactly where they are."

"Oh, *really?* And just how do you know that, Christopher Columbia?"

Matt grabbed the back of Radar's head and turned it, facing him toward the city.

"Look at the lights," Matt said.

Radar was silent for a moment - only a moment - and said, "Very pretty, but that don't—"

"Shut up!" Matt pulled Radar to his feet and pointed at the city. "Look at them. Look at how they're arranged. Anything funny about those lights?"

Radar shrugged and shook his head. "You mean besides the obvious?"

"Remember Las Vegas? Everything was lit up. *Everything.* Now what's so different about these lights?"

107

Suddenly the anger disappeared from Radar's eyes, and they widened with realization, "The streets. Only the streets are lit up. The buildings are all dark."

Matt shook his head. "Not all of 'em. See that tight cluster toward the center?"

Sure enough, Radar saw a tall building with lights burning on nearly every floor surrounded by a tight cluster of smaller buildings that were also illuminated.

Matt pointed at the cluster of lit buildings. "I'll bet you a gallon of crystal clear that's where your pirate friends are headed."

Radar's shoulders slumped. "They're not pirates. They're a private army."

Matt nodded. "Sure looks that way."

"So what do we do now?"

"We find someplace to stash the car and wait until morning. Those streets are lit for security. If we go rolling in there now, they'll be all over us, and my car will wind up parked right next to your truck."

"So we go native?"

"Yeah. We go native."

Without another word, the wellers walked back to the car. As he reached his door, Matt stopped and looked over the roof at his friend.

"Oh, and Radar?"

"Yeah?"

"It's Christopher *Columbo*, you ignorant ass."

# Eighteen

Shortly after dawn, the wellers ventured out of an abandoned service station on the southern edge of the city. The Road Runner lay hidden within one of the empty bays, right next to a rust-encrusted minivan still raised up on a hoist and completely drained of oil. The rising sun, blinding and hot, was comforting to the seasoned wastelanders. It was familiar to them, unlike the enigmatic city lights that had plagued their sleep. Radar's sleep, anyway.

Of course Matt had slept, because he knew his friend, the constant worrier, would not. Paranoia bred fantastic watchdogs. So even though Radar was bleary-eyed and jittery, Matt was rested and alert.

Radar yawned as he scooped a heaping sporkful of spaghetti rings from the can in his hand and shoveled the red mess into his mouth. Matt reached into his own and plucked out a green bean, then glanced longingly at his friend's breakfast before popping the soggy vegetable into his mouth.

"So," said Radar, scraping the bottom of his can with his spork, "how do we want to do this?"

Matt nodded toward the northeast. "I saw some fires off in that direction last night. Seems like as good a place as any. When we get there, remember, we're traders, not wellers."

Radar licked his spork clean. "*Again...* I got it. What are we trading?"

Matt patted the canvas pack hanging at his side. "Batteries, perfume, and wet naps."

"We've got wet naps?" Radar tossed his empty can into some nearby weeds. "Give me one!"

Matt smiled and popped another green bean into his mouth. "You can't afford it."

"Consider it a loan until I get my stuff—"

A noise in the weeds, barely louder than a whisper, caught the tall weller's attention. Radar dropped to one knee and pulled a .38 from his boot, leveling it at the patch of weeds. Simultaneously, Matt's hand shot beneath his coat, his fingers closing around the Well Digger's wooden grip. His eyes narrowed against the rising sun as he surveyed the weeds. For a moment, neither of them moved, nor did they breathe. The only sound was the cool morning breeze rustling through the brush.

"Matt?" Radar whispered.

*"Cover me,"* Matt mouthed silently.

Matt placed his can on the ground and slowly drew his machete. Staying low, he crept toward the edge of the weeds, the blade held out in front of him. As he came within striking distance of the foliage, he looked over his shoulder at Radar. Radar nodded and quietly cocked back the hammer on his revolver.

Quick as lightning, Matt swung the machete in a long arc, neatly cleaving the dry plant matter. There, nestled in the weeds, with one hand shoved deep into Radar's discarded pasta can, was a small boy. He bolted out of the brush, but Matt snatched him up by the back of his coat with his left hand. He lifted the kicking child into the air.

The boy's clothes were much too large for him, his pants secured with several lengths of pieced-together baling twine. His shoes, whose soles were falling off, were held together the same way. His eyes were wild and frightened, but a cracked respirator mask covered the lower half of his face and muffled his cries of protest. Despite his struggling, he held on tight to the empty can.

Matt reached for the boy's mask. "Calm down!"

The boy struggled all the more aggressively, apparently determined to keep Matt's hands away.

Radar snorted and lowered his gun. "Lookit that. He doesn't like being told to calm down either."

Matt cast a sideways glance and rolled his eyes. He returned his gaze to the boy and the can still clutched tightly in his grimy fingers.

Matt sheathed the machete and held out his hand. "Hand me the beans."

Radar hesitantly complied. "We feeding strays now?"

"Why not? I'm feeding you, ain't I?" Matt took the can and offered it to the flailing child. "Hey! Kid! Lookit me! Hungry?"

The boy instantly became still, his eyes fixated on the can of beans. The empty pasta can fell from his hand, revealing a smattering of tomato sauce on his skin. The only sound was the clatter of aluminum on concrete.

"That's better," said Matt. "You speak English?"

The boy nodded, his mask bobbing up and down comically.

"Good." Matt reached for the boy's mask. "Now I'm gonna take this off, and we're going to have us a little chat. All right?"

The boy nodded.

Matt carefully pulled the boy's mask up onto his forehead, exposing a filthy mouth ringed with food and dirt resembling a clown's painted smile. The boy no longer looked wild, merely indifferent, as if he were used to trading obedience for food.

"What's your name?"

The boy hesitated, but finally answered, "Collin."

"Collin." Matt nodded in greeting. "My name's Matt, and this is Radar."

Radar offered a smarmy wave. "Hello."

Collin looked briefly at Radar, then back to Matt. "Can I have the beans now, mister?"

"Matt," the weller corrected him. "Here you go."

The boy took the can and looked at Matt expectantly.

"If I put you down, you going to run away?" Matt asked.

Collin shook his head; he looked sincere enough. Matt placed the boy on the ground and watched as he quickly scooped several green beans into his mouth at a time, chewing only once or twice before swallowing.

"So, Collin, where do you live?" Matt asked.

The boy didn't stop eating, but merely jerked his head over his right shoulder.

"Thatta way, huh? Lotta people?"

Collin shrugged.

Matt found the boy's noncommittal answers trying, but he did his best to sound upbeat. "Well, see, we're traders, and we—"

"You ain't traders," Collin said between bites. "You're wellers."

Matt tried not to look shocked. "What gave you that idea?"

The boy opened his mouth to speak, but Radar beat him to the punch. "Your voice carries."

Matt gritted his teeth and hissed. "Thank you, *Scott.*"

Radar grinned. "You're welcome, Matthew."

"Look, Collin." Matt placed a hand on the boy's shoulder. "No more bullshit. My friend had something taken from him, and we're looking for the men who took it. Men in cars. Do you know where we can find them?"

"Duh." Colin fished out the final green bean and tossed the can away. "Them's Koozy's men."

"Koozy? Can you take me to them?"

Collin shook his head and pulled his respirator down over his mouth and nose, muffling his speech. "No way, mister!"

Matt sighed. "Well, can you take me to somebody who can?"

Collin shrugged and turned to leave, motioning for the wellers to follow him.

After a few steps, Radar's curiosity got the better of him. "Hey, kid! What's with the mask?"

"Bad air," the boy replied. "Duh."

The wellers exchanged brief glances and quickly tied their bandanas over their faces.

# Nineteen

As they walked, Matt began to notice a difference in the air the farther they pressed into the city. Even through the bandana it seemed thicker, muggier, as though it were pressing down upon him. All the kid had said was that the air was "bad," but what gave it such an oppressive weight?

As they walked, it took on another quality. Through his crude filter Matt could smell the telltale odors of people. Poverty, it turned out, really did have a scent. Collin pushed through a thick wall of shrubbery and broke through into what Matt assumed must have been a suburb at one time. The street was lined with dilapidated houses, some with their two-car garages on the left and others on the right, but for the most part, the dwellings were indistinguishable from one another.

Some of the garages were open, with makeshift counters and workbenches serving as symbols of commerce. The locals milled around in the street, some going about their daily routines, others chatting up the shopkeepers. Matt noticed that they all seemed dirtier than most villagers he'd encountered in his travels - younger too. Most of them were female, but that didn't really surprise him. The men were most likely performing labor elsewhere.

They all did share two common traits that Matt could see, however. They all wore some type of air filter over their faces, and they all looked-

"Pretty sickly," said Radar. "Ain't they?"

Matt nodded. "I don't like it."

Radar tugged on his bandana. "Am I the only one that feels underdressed for this party?"

Matt had a gas mask, but it was stowed away in the Road Runner's trunk. *Survival fail*, his grandfather would have said.

An old woman selling shriveled vegetables from the trunk of a derelict sedan coughed through her respirator, and then lifted the mask and spat blood onto the asphalt. "Outlanders!" she croaked.

"Uh oh," said Radar.

Others nearby soon took up the crone's feeble cry as they took note of the wellers' presence. This was the part Matt always dreaded, that awkward moment when you didn't know if the locals were going to lift you up onto their shoulders or roast you on a spit. His fingers brushed the edge of his coat, ready to reach beneath for the Well Digger at a moment's notice. A crowd began to gather and encircle them and their young guide.

Matt swallowed the growing lump in his throat, along with his fear and said, in as cheerful a voice as possible, "Mornin'!"

The crowd halted their advance, keeping a respectful distance from the outlanders. One of the women in the back called out in a muffled voice, "What's yer business, outlander?"

Matt smiled behind his bandana. "We're here to tra—"

"They're wellers," said Collin.

Matt ground his teeth and exchanged a nervous glance with Radar. This was the point where negotiations sometimes went south.

"Our water supply's fine," croaked an old man standing near Radar.

"Glad to hear it," said Matt. "We're still lookin' to trade."

After a few brief moments of mumbling amongst the locals, a female voice rose above the din, "Whatcha got, stranger?"

"Perfume, wet naps, and batteries."

"You got D cells?" another female voice called out excitedly.

114

Matt nodded. "Yes, ma'am, I do."

A jovial male voice rang out, "Well we all know what Karen wants those for!"

The crowd erupted into laughter. Matt looked over at Radar; his eyes conveyed the same sense of relief. The hard part was over. With the tension broken, the crowd began to move in on the wellers in a less ominous fashion, each person eager to broker a deal with them.

Matt opened his bag and prepared to present his wares when someone called out, "Hold up! Any outside traders have to be approved by the mayor!"

"Fair enough." Matt closed his pack. "Where do I find him?"

"*She* is right here."

The crowd parted to Matt's left, revealing a black woman in a gas mask and a gun on her left hip that might have been the Well Digger's single-barreled little brother. The mayor appraised the wellers for a moment and then walked toward them, dragging her right foot slightly. Matt could tell by her posture and the iron she carried that the limp wasn't a "gift" from God, but the mark of a warrior. This woman had walked into Hell and limped out its master.

He liked her already.

When the woman reached them, she peeled the gas mask off, exposing her stifled face to the air. She paused a moment to relish the sensation on her sweat-spotted skin as she shook out her braids.

Before Matt realized he was staring, the mayor said, "Draw a picture, outlander. It'll last longer."

Matt pulled his bandana down around his neck and held out his hand. "Name's Matt. This here is Radar."

Radar cocked an eyebrow and gave the mayor a two-fingered salute.

The mayor looked back and forth between the two men for a moment before accepting Matt's hand. "Phoenix."

"Phoenix?" Matt shook her hand. "I like that. Reminds me of home."

"Didn't you run away from home?" Radar asked.

"Shut up, Radar," Matt hissed through gritted teeth.

Phoenix turned and walked away. "Come with me."

Matt adjusted the heavy pack's strap on his shoulder and trudged up a cracked driveway behind Phoenix, trying hard to keep his eyes off her ass as she walked. Radar fell into step beside him, breaking the spell cast by Phoenix's backside.

"I wouldn't mind drinking from her well," Radar whispered.

Without looking back or breaking her stride, Phoenix gave Radar the finger. Matt smirked. The driveway led to a mold-covered house with large panels of plywood nailed over the undoubtedly broken bay window. The wellers followed Phoenix up the crumbling concrete steps and into the dim house.

Despite the dust and cobwebs, Matt was surprised by the dwelling's condition. The house lacked the typical signs of post-war habitation: debris, graffiti and broken windows; the front window was the obvious exception. Phoenix led them into an office at the back and sat behind a warped wooden desk, immediately resting her dirt-encrusted boots on top of it. Matt suppressed a laugh; even in this age of death and decay, a desk still commanded respect for the person sitting behind it. Personally, he preferred his symbols of power to be portable, chrome, and loaded.

He took in his surroundings, an instinctual action that had saved his life on more occasions than he could count. The room was sparsely, but comfortably furnished. The mayor's desk sat in front of the only window, keeping her in silhouette, a sad-looking blue couch rested against the opposite end and a large drafting table filled a corner. The walls were covered in faded posters and curled pieces of hand-drawn artwork. A framed photograph above the drafting table, however, caught Matt's eye.

Through the thick coating of dust on the glass, he could make out a smiling family. A mother and father knelt beside a young boy in a baseball cap and a red-haired little girl clutching a stuffed giraffe. A small dog - some kind of curly-haired mutt - stood with its front paws on the boy's shoulder. Phoenix followed Matt's gaze to the photograph.

"The previous owners," Phoenix explained. "My granddaddy found this place abandoned after the war and moved in with my mama and aunts."

"Why do you keep the picture?" Radar asked.

Phoenix chuckled. "My granddaddy kept it. He thought it was a showing of thanks for leaving us such a beautiful home. It used to be anyway, until Koozy..."

There was that name again. "Koozy?" Matt asked.

Phoenix tore her eyes away from the portrait. She ignored the question. "So, what do not one, but two wellers want in my 'fair city?' You don't honestly expect me to believe you came here to *trade*, do you?"

"Oh, we're here to trade all right," said Matt. "We need information."

Phoenix raised an eyebrow. "Information?"

"You mentioned a name."

Phoenix's lip curled in disgust. "Koozy."

Matt nodded.

Phoenix removed her boots from the desk and sat up. The chair creaked loudly. "What about him?"

Matt jerked a thumb at Radar. "We think he has something that belongs to my friend here."

"Then it's gone," said Phoenix matter-of-factly.

"We'll see."

"Look," said Phoenix, "Patrick Koozy may be some sleaze in a suit, but he owns every inch of ground from Des Moines to the Mississippi, and that private army of his keeps it that way. If you go up against him, you're going to wind up dead. Or worse."

Dead, or worse. Matt loved that particular cliche. Wastelanders were particularly fond of it. He smirked.

"You don't believe me?" asked Phoenix.

Matt opened his mouth to speak, but Radar beat him to the punch. "Lady, where we come from, we have a reputation. Back home, we are 'or worse.'"

Matt cast his companion a sideways glance. "Radar?"

"Yeah, Matt?"

"Shut up."

"Yessum."

ADAM J. WHITLATCH

"*Gentlemen*," said Phoenix, "if you want to go up against Patrick Koozy, that's your business. He ain't hard to find. But I won't put any of my people in harm's way just for a couple of outlanders."

"We don't plan on getting anyone hurt, Phoenix," said Matt. "We just want information. That's all. You talk, we pay, and we leave."

Phoenix sat back, causing her chair to squawk again. "Fair enough. Ask."

"The lights. How does Koozy pull that off?"

"You ever seen a steam engine, outlander?"

He'd seen several. Most recently, he'd seen a few during his search of Fort Frontier. You didn't often see them in operation, however, due to the necessary component. If Koozy was using steam power to light an entire city, he would need an endless water supply.

"Where's he get the water?" Matt asked.

"He pipes it in from the Cedar River up north in Cedar Rapids," Phoenix explained. "It's too contaminated to use for anything else."

Radar quickly pulled the bandana back over his face and pulled Matt in close. "Nuke water!" he hissed.

Matt shook his head and whispered, "The boiling process would leave the fallout behind. It wouldn't go into the air."

"You *think!*"

"I think." Matt pulled the Geiger counter from his pack.

"Matt, these people are all sick! God only knows what else is in that water!"

Matt nodded. He turned on the counter and listened, but the clicking didn't register any dangerous levels of radiation. He breathed a sigh of relief. Unfortunately, that only created more questions. Any number of chemicals could have been put into the air by the steam engines. Or...

"You said you *don't* use that water for drinking?" Matt turned to Phoenix.

Phoenix shook her head. "We get our water from the Iowa River. Besides, we filter and boil it to be safe."

"So Koozy's not dipping into his drinking water for his power source."

"Not *his* drinking water." Phoenix corrected.

118

Something in the mayor's tone bothered Matt. "What do you mean?"

Phoenix became silent.

"Phoenix?" Matt placed his hands on her desk and leaned in. "Where does Koozy get his drinking water?"

Radar's body suddenly tensed, and he cocked his head to the north. "Matt!"

Matt looked over his shoulder, first annoyed, but then alarmed by his friend's expression. His left hand instinctively moved to his hip.

Phoenix stood. "What is it?"

Radar's head turned, as if following some sound the others could not hear, which, Matt knew, was *exactly* what he was doing. "We're about to have company," Radar murmured.

"The culling," said Phoenix. "Shit!"

Before Matt could ask for clarification, Phoenix stormed past them toward the front door. Matt pulled on his bandana and followed. As they stepped outside, he could finally hear the sound of engines approaching from the north. All around them, villagers ran for cover, pushing and shoving each other out of the way. Matt was beginning to get a good idea of what Phoenix had meant by "the culling."

He hoped he was wrong.

A pair of vehicles, a familiar-looking dune buggy and a graffiti-covered moving truck, turned the corner, and shots rang out. The gunfire brought the townsfolk to an immediate and obedient halt. They stood still, their heads bowed, eyes cast at the ground. Only Phoenix and the two outlanders dared to look upon the vehicles coming to a screeching halt in the middle of the street.

The dune buggy's two occupants hopped out and surveyed the fear-stricken townspeople. Their rifles were pointed skyward, ready to fire warning shots if anyone stepped out of line. They didn't realize the mistake they were making.

Matt Freeborn didn't believe in warning shots.

The driver of the truck walked to the rear and rolled the door open.

"I need volunteers," one of the men said. His voice was muffled by his gas mask.

No one spoke.

The man removed his mask and Matt instantly recognized him. These were the very same pirates they'd followed into town the night before.

"I *said*, I need volunteers!" the pirate bellowed

The request was answered with frightened whimpers. Matt watched as the pirate approached the old vegetable merchant. The pirate ripped the woman's respirator off her face with enough force to throw her to the ground.

"Take this one," the pirate said. "She's half dead anyhow."

"No!" the old woman shrieked. "Please, no!"

"The culling," Matt whispered to Phoenix. "Distillers?"

Phoenix nodded.

"I hate distillers," said Radar. "Bad for business."

That wasn't how Matt would have put it. *Ghoulish* was more like it, but his sentiment was the same. The world was too damned small for distillers and wellers to breathe the same air.

"Take 'em?" asked Radar.

Matt pulled his bandana down. "Take 'em."

Chrome flashed in the morning sun, and the pirates found themselves covered by the wellers' revolvers. The leader brought his rifle around, ready to fire from the hip.

Before the pirate's finger touched the trigger, Matt fired the Well Digger and vaporized the man's head. The air trembled with its roar, causing the other pirates to hesitate long enough for Radar to put two rounds into the dune buggy's passenger. Matt dropped to one knee and shot the truck driver in the arm, taking it clean off above the elbow.

It was all over in seconds.

For a moment, the only sounds were the wounded man's cries and the thunderous echo of the Well Digger's report. The townspeople stood in stunned silence, all eyes on the wellers and their smoking weapons.

"What the hell have you *done*?" one of the villagers shouted. Matt looked at the speaker, at the mixed expression of fear and anger on his face.

"You're welcome," said Radar.

"You fools!" the man wailed. "You've killed us all. Koozy will send his entire army here."

The outrage was infectious, spreading through the crowd like a plague.

Matt was silent. Radar, however, rarely was, and this was no exception.

"What's wrong with you people?" he shouted. "Do you like being cattle for the *rich?*" He spat the last word as if it carried a foul taste.

"What *choice* do we have?"

"What choice?" Radar said incredulously. "Leave! Just leave!"

"And go where?" asked Phoenix. "Patrick Koozy owns the roads. We wouldn't make it five miles."

"She's right!" a weak voice called out.

The crowd turned to look at the wounded truck driver, who was struggling along the ground, blood pooling beneath his body. Matt holstered the Well Digger and walked toward him, weaving around townsfolk like a shark through water.

"You're all dead!" The pirate sneered. "Koozy owns the road, he owns this town, he owns you... *all* of you! Even *you*, outlander!"

Matt towered over the pirate. "That right?"

"You bet your ass!" The pirate laughed. "Round here... Koozy's *God*!"

"Funny thing..." Matt lifted the pirate up by his lapels and threw him against the grille of the truck. "In all my years, I've met 'God' at least a dozen times. And do you know what I learned from each of those holy encounters?"

The pirate's jaw tensed.

"*God*..." Matt drew his machete. "He bleeds just like everyone else. Just like *you*."

The pirate screamed, but the sound was cut off as the machete sliced through the man's neck. Matt flicked blood from the blade as the head rolled under the truck. He turned and looked at the townspeople, who looked more afraid than ever. He sheathed the weapon and walked through them; they parted for him like the Red Sea.

As he approached Radar and Phoenix, the mayor clapped slowly. There was no appreciation in the applause. Each clap sounded like a coffin nail being driven home.

"Well," said Phoenix. "Thank you *very* much.

Matt ignored her and approached Radar. The tall weller took a deep breath and surveyed the damage. Matt could see the doubt and regret on his friend's face. It would pass. It always did.

Matt looked Phoenix in the eyes, two burning coals of hate. "We need a guide into the city."

"Forget it."

"They'll be coming for you now. All of you."

"And whose fault is that?" Phoenix snapped. "*Outlander.*"

"Will it matter?" Matt countered. "Do you think Koozy gives a good goddamn who pulled the trigger?"

Phoenix averted her gaze, but Matt stepped right back into view.

"I can end this," Matt said, his tone soft but resolved. "Trust me."

Phoenix took a step closer, their noses almost touching. "I don't have to *trust* you, outlander. *You* brought this down on us, so *you* fix it."

Matt nodded. He turned and walked away, with Radar close on his heels.

"What's the plan, Matt?"

Matt pointed at the pirate leader's corpse. "Strip him. Take his mask and armor."

While Radar went about his task, Matt went to work on the other pirate. With luck, Koozy's men wouldn't realize they were a man short. Unfortunately, along with warning shots, Matt Freeborn also didn't believe in luck.

# Twenty

The old truck rumbled over the broken asphalt, and Matt squirmed in the driver's seat as a broken spring poked him in the ass. Ahead of him, Radar drove the stolen dune buggy, following the well-worn path through the grass and weeds taking root. The extra moisture in the air from Koozy's generators seemed to be doing the local vegetation some good, even if it didn't do much for the human population. Matt was glad to have some protection, having stripped Koozy's foot soldiers of their masks, but the damn respirator smelled like a dead cat's asshole, and the pirate's armor was too tight.

The dune buggy came to an abrupt stop at an intersection, and Matt stomped on the brake pedal. Unfortunately the brakes on the old truck were almost nonexistent, and it slammed into the back of the buggy, throwing Radar against the steering wheel. Radar stood and ripped off his mask; Matt could see murder in his friend's eyes.

Matt stuck his head out the window. "Sorry!"

Radar hopped out of the buggy and stomped toward the truck. "Dammit, didn't your granddaddy teach you what the pedal on the left is for?"

"Sure." Matt grinned behind his mask. "Blondes."

Radar shook his head and laughed. "I hate you."

"Why'd you stop?"

"The road splits, and the tracks go in all directions. We can't just wander around like tourists. One wrong turn and anybody watching will know something's wrong."

Matt sighed. Radar was right. They really didn't know where they were going. North, of course, but they were still several miles from the building they'd seen the night before.

Radar crossed his arms. "Well?"

"I'm thinking!" Matt snapped.

"Don't hurt yourself," a voice said.

The passenger-side door opened, and Matt readied his weapon, but quickly lowered it as Phoenix climbed into the cab and shut the door. She was wearing stolen pirate armor, but still wore her own gas mask. A drab green bandana covered her braids.

"Hello," she said cheerfully, obviously proud of her ability to sneak up on not one, but two wellers.

Matt turned back to Radar. "You couldn't hear her comin'?"

Radar patted the truck. "Knocking rocker arm, leaky manifold, frayed serp belt, bent fan bla—"

Matt held up a hand. "All right, shut up. You're useless."

"Your mother didn't think so."

Radar may not have heard the mayor's arrival, but Matt made sure he heard the Well Digger's hammer cocking.

*"Gentlemen,"* Phoenix used her mayor voice. "As much as I hate to admit it, I need you, and you're not going to get very far without me. So, like it or not, I'm stuck with you. I can get you through the city safely *without* driving over any mines."

*"Mines?"* Radar shouted.

"So," Phoenix continued, "just go where I tell you and we'll all get to watch the sunset tonight."

"Sounds romantic," Radar said.

Phoenix looked at Matt. "You *like* hanging out with this guy?"

"Well, generally no," Matt admitted. "But Koozy's men took his wheels. The sooner we get his truck back, the sooner we part ways."

"And you two get the hell out of my town?"

Matt nodded.

"Fine," said Phoenix. "Turn right here, follow the tracks for six blocks, then—"

"Uh," Matt interrupted. "It might work better if you rode with Radar. He *is* in the lead car."

Radar blew into his hand to check his breath and wagged his eyebrows at the mayor. Phoenix looked at Matt pleadingly, but he simply shrugged. Phoenix got out and followed Radar to the buggy. Radar held out his hand to help her into the vehicle and, over the truck's engine, Matt could barely hear her say, "Just keep your hands to yourself, outlander. You don't need your dick to drive."

Matt smiled as he put the truck in gear. He wasn't too sure about Phoenix's observation. He'd seen Radar drive; there had to be *some* explanation for it.

*****

They passed several other pirate vehicles along the way. If Koozy's men saw through their disguises, they didn't show it. Houses gave way to ruined and abandoned businesses, which in turn were replaced by tall office buildings. These structures always made Matt nervous. He always imagined he heard their supports creaking in the wind, as if they could come crumbling down on top of him at any moment.

The haze in the air was much thicker now, and he actually had to turn on the windshield wipers to clear the moisture. The sidewalks were lined with workers, some of whom were carrying crates and boxes, but others were lugging bundles of wood into a warehouse through a loading dock. Steam billowed out from a hole in the roof.

In the buggy, Radar pointed at the power plant, then closed and opened his fist. *Kaboom!*

Matt nodded. All in good time.

Suddenly Radar held up his fist. Matt took his foot off the gas and pulled the hand brake, not wanting to slam into the buggy in the middle of the street. Radar turned into an alley beside the power plant, and Matt followed. Radar gave the signal to stop about halfway down, and Matt set the truck's parking brake.

ADAM J. WHITLATCH

He watched as Phoenix got out and knocked on a steel door set into the side of the power plant; a few seconds later a man answered. Matt could see that he was perspiring heavily. He nodded to Phoenix and looked at Matt, his cue to get out. As they followed the man to the back of the truck, Radar pulled a stolen hunting knife from his jacket and pressed the flat of the blade against his leg; he nodded to Matt.

*Ready.*

Matt returned the nod.

"How many?" the distiller asked.

"Uh, three," Matt replied.

"Not more old fucks, I hope," the man grumbled. "They don't yield enough to be worth the trouble."

"Oh no," Matt assured him. "These are three strapping young lads."

The man waited while Matt raised the door. Within, the corpses of the three pirates lay side by side. The truck driver's head, however, had rolled toward the front of the truck. Matt followed the man up inside.

"Oh, what the *fuck?*" the man howled. "They're dead!"

Matt shrugged. "They resisted."

"Bleeding wastes moisture," the distiller scolded. "How many times do I have to tell ya?"

Matt looked down at his feet, feigning shame.

The man knelt beside the closest corpse and rolled it over. "Wait a min- This is Rotgut!"

"Er, well—" Matt stuttered, pulling Radar up into the truck.

"And this is Thrasher!" the man exclaimed. He whirled on the two wellers. "You're not—"

Matt drew the Well Digger and struck the top of the man's head with the butt, then grabbed his limp body and tossed him around to Radar. Radar's knife flashed, and hot blood painted the inside of the truck. Matt kicked the dying man toward the front, and the wellers jumped out. Matt pulled the door down behind him.

"Not bad," Phoenix said.

"Thank you," said Radar, wiping his knife clean on his pant leg.

126

"Where to now?" asked Matt.

"This is as far as I've ever been," Phoenix admitted.

"Then we play it by ear. Come on."

Matt led the way through the open doorway and into a narrow hallway, leading with the Well Digger. The air was filled with the cacophony of clanking machines and oppressive humidity. At the end was a stairwell going up and down. Matt checked to make sure it was clear before motioning the others inside.

"Where to?" he whispered.

"My gut says down," said Radar.

Matt nodded. "Mine too. Let's go."

They descended the stairs quickly, the constant din of machinery negating the need for stealth. When they reached the door at the bottom, Matt pulled it open only a few inches, peering inside. Satisfied that the coast was clear, he looked at Radar and jerked his head forward.

"I'll cover you," Matt whispered.

Radar nodded and slipped through. Matt watched until Radar signaled for him to follow, then did so, with Phoenix right behind him.

The room was dimly lit, and lined with cages of chain link, the wire rusted from the moisture in the air. Matt didn't scare easily, but this place was giving him the creeps. At the end of the cages, he could see a light burning from around the corner. The sound of rattling chains made the hairs on the back of his neck stand up.

He could tell Radar was as wired as he was, probably more so. Distillers were the boogeymen of the wastes, and probably the only thing a weller truly feared. In the years following the war, distilling had curbed a significant problem, and had been a necessary evil. But over time the practice fell out of favor as it ceased to address the needs of the masses, and instead fulfilled the desires of the rich.

Distillers became the new vampires of the post-nuclear world, often snatching the weak and defenseless from their beds in the night. Matt's grandfather had told him about the distillers one night by the fire. He'd confessed that once - only once - in the early days after the war, he'd drunk the "water of the dead." When Matt, young and wide-eyed, had asked him what the water tasted like, the old man answered with a single chilling and damning word.

*Death.*

Patrick Koozy wasn't a god. He was a devil.

"Help me!" a voice rasped.

Matt whipped around toward the source. He reached for his gun, but Phoenix stopped him with a touch on the arm. She crept up to the wall of chain link to their left, peering into the darkness.

Slowly, a gaunt face emerged from the gloom. A long, gray beard hung from the man's bony chin. He slipped his filthy fingers through the holes in the fence.

Phoenix knelt in front of the cage and ripped the gas mask off her face. "Samuel!"

The prisoner perked up. "Phoenix!"

"This is Samuel Morris," Phoenix explained. "Koozy's men took him last week. Samuel, is anyone else still alive?"

He shook his head. "I'm the last. My God, Phoenix, the screams! *The screams!*"

Matt shuddered. He knew what the old man was trying to say. The screams of a living being, human or otherwise - he'd witnessed the procedure being done to animals as well, and it was no less horrific - being sucked dry was enough to make even the hardest man piss himself.

"You've got to get me out of here!" Samuel pleaded.

"We will." Phoenix turned to the wellers. "Can you—"

Radar nudged Phoenix aside and went to work on the lock with his knife. It was rusty, but still strong enough to resist the knife. The blade snapped and clattered to the wet concrete floor. Samuel sobbed.

"Hold on," Radar said. "I'll go find something else."

"Be careful," Matt hissed as his friend disappeared around the corner.

Matt took a deep breath, but nearly choked on it as a blood-curdling scream filled the room.

Matt drew the Well Digger. "Radar!"

Matt rounded the corner into a larger room and tripped, tumbling to the slimy floor. He panicked as his limbs became entwined with someone else. Finally he recognized the freakishly long arm as Radar's. He had tripped over his friend's trembling body.

"Ya damn idjit!" Matt growled. "What the hell is wrong with—"

Then he saw it. Looming above them, propped in a corner against the wall, was what at first glance looked like a mummy.

The corpse was gray and shriveled; the cracked and flaking flesh clung tightly to the skeleton underneath. Its bony fingers clutched the air, the nails hanging by a thread, exposing the tips. Most terrifying of all, however, was the face. The lips were gone, drawn back to expose a maw locked in an agonizing scream, and black, hollow sockets stared pleadingly toward Heaven; tiny white globules deep inside were all that remained of the eyes.

Matt closed his eyes, but when he opened them, the corpse was still there, shrieking silently. He tore his gaze away from the horror, but saw another corpse nearby, this one still locked into the extraction machine. It even still had the needles imbedded in its fragile skin. A nearby tank held nearly ten gallons of crystal clear water. Matt watched as a fat drop fell into the tank, creating ripples.

"Mattie..." Radar whispered. He hadn't called his friend Mattie since they were children.

Matt gasped, suddenly realizing he'd been holding his breath. He nodded, his eyes still on the mummies. "Yeah?"

"Let's get the fuck outta here."

Matt felt along the ground until he found Radar's hand, still soft, pliable, and full of life. And water. He patted his hand reassuringly. "Sure, buddy."

As Matt helped Radar to his feet, a distant sound made them freeze. Whistling, accompanied by brisk footsteps, emanated from an adjoining corridor.

"Someone's coming," Phoenix hissed.

"Hide!" Matt whispered, shoving Radar toward the hallway of cages where Phoenix and Samuel waited.

Matt and Radar crouched in the shadows and waited, until finally a man stepped into the extraction room. He was short, dressed in a filthy lab coat that hadn't been white in decades and wore a cracked pair of black-rimmed reading glasses over his beady eyes. His shrill whistling echoed off the damp cement walls. When he came to the corpse in the machine, he stopped whistling, bringing the tune to a whimsical, high-pitched end.

"Hello, Mrs. Morris!" the distiller said cheerfully. "All done, are we?"

At the mention of his wife, Samuel let out a pitiful moan. Matt tensed.

"Patience, Mr. Morris," the distiller called. "Your turn is coming."

Matt watched as the distiller removed the water tank from the extractor, sealed it and replaced it with an empty one.

Matt felt Radar's hot breath in his ear, barely a whisper. "I'm going to blow this motherfucker's head off!"

Matt held up a hand. *Wait!*

The distiller went to work on freeing Mrs. Morris from the machine, retracting the hypodermic needles with the pull of a lever. He pushed a second one, and the restraints holding the body up also withdrew, allowing it to fall forward. He caught the body and laughed, pulling it into a close embrace. Matt felt the green beans he'd had for breakfast beginning to rise as the distiller waltzed around the room with the crumbling mummy.

Radar held up his .38. "Now?"

*Not yet*, Matt mouthed.

The distiller thrust the corpse into the corner with the other, and then bowed low to his crumbling partner. One of Mrs. Morris' arms fell off at the elbow, and the distiller quickly bent to retrieve it. "A token? Milady flatters me."

"Now?" Radar hissed.

Matt cocked the Well Digger. "Allow *me!*"

"Mr. Morris?" the distiller called out as he made his way to the cages. "Are you ready to join your blushing bride?"

As the distiller rounded the corner, he felt the Well Digger's cold barrels pressed underneath his chin, then the barrel of Radar's .38 against his temple.

"Don't make a goddamned sound," said Matt, trying to keep his voice level. His head was swimming with conflicted feelings of rage, disgust, sadness, and fear.

"Who are you people?" the distiller demanded.

Radar cocked back the hammer and drove the barrel harder into the man's skull. "Shut. The fuck. *Up!*"

Matt held out his hand. "The key to the cage."

The distiller stared defiantly, his nostrils flared.

Matt disengaged the lower safety, ready to unload both barrels into the man's skull. "Now!"

The distiller fished a ring of keys from his coat pocket, and Matt snatched them up. He tossed them to Phoenix.

"Get him out of there," he said. "And hurry."

"You'll never leave here alive!" the distiller threatened.

"Funny," said Radar. "I was just thinking the same thing about *you.*"

The cage door creaked open, and Phoenix went to work on the chains binding Samuel's hands. When he was finally free, Phoenix had to hold him back to keep him from wringing the distiller's neck, although Matt couldn't fathom why she didn't let him go. He soon gave up and collapsed into her arms. He sobbed, tears streaking his filthy face.

"Oh, please don't," the distiller whined. "You're wasting water!" He laughed - a sound somewhere between a hyena and deranged child. Obviously the screams had destroyed what little humanity and brains this man had long ago. He was crazy as a shithouse rat.

Matt clamped his right hand around the distiller's throat with enough force to knock his head back and send his glasses up onto his forehead. He guided the gasping lunatic through the extraction room and slammed him into the machine. His grip tightened on his hostage's throat.

He nodded toward the levers on the machine. "Radar."

Radar approached, his eyes locked on the distiller's as he pulled the lever for the restraints. Steel bands enveloped the distiller's wrists, waist and legs. The distiller looked at Matt, his eyes wild, but the weller's expression was stone cold. Radar pushed up on the second lever, and thirty hypodermic needles jabbed into the man's body from all angles, including two thick spikes that bored through the skull and brain.

The distiller screamed and bucked, but his struggles paled in comparison to what happened when Radar pressed the green button on the side of the machine. The distiller's panicked cries changed into otherworldly shrieks, his features contorted in unimaginable agony. Matt's face twitched as they filled the room and bored into his ear canals like steel claws, but he forced himself to watch.

The man's cheeks sunk like deflated balloons, and his clothes hung loose on his frame as his stomach, arms, and legs lost their mass. The eyes, wide with terror, clouded over and began to shrivel, retreating deep into the dark recesses of their sockets. The lips, all color removed from them, thinned out, split, and were pulled back from the yellow teeth, two of which fell out as the gums dried up. As the tongue withered away, the unearthly yells faded into a groaning wheeze.

The nose and ears shriveled away, allowing the reading glasses to fall to the floor and shatter. The skeletal head moved slowly back and forth, the blind sockets staring pleadingly at the wellers until, finally, the muscles in the neck lost all pliancy and the skin began to crumble. The fingers curled as the tendons dried up and tightened, leaving the hands as grasping, bony claws. With a final, rattling breath, the thing became still and eerily silent.

For a minute, the only sound in the room was the steady *drip-drip-drip* of water into the collection tank. All eyes were locked on the twisted, skeletal husk that only minutes ago had been a living, breathing human being. Samuel limped into the room, and the wellers stood aside as he approached the machine. The old man reeled back and spat right on the distilled man's face, but the saliva was immediately absorbed by the flaking flesh, leaving no trace, like a drop of rain on the desert sands.

Radar crossed the room to a cluttered worktable and rummaged through the toolboxes until he found a rusty pipe wrench. He swung it at the machine, crushing the distiller's skull and snapping off the hypodermics. The wrench came down on the machine again, and again, and again, until nothing remained but a frame of twisted metal, broken tubing, and a pile of dust and bones.

His shoulders heaved, and his breath came in ragged gasps as he looked upon his handiwork. He tossed the wrench to the ground at the base of the machine, scattering what remained of the distiller's skeleton.

"Let's get the hell out of here," Radar said. He turned. "Matt?"

# Twenty-One

Matt was already walking toward the exit. When he reached the stairwell, he took the steps two at a time, ignoring his companions' pleas to slow down.

*Run, Mattie! Don't look back!*

At the top, Matt broke into a jog, eager to get out of this building, out of this town - hell, he'd settle for off this planet with those star people from Radar's fantasies.

The image of the drained distiller was burned into his brain, painted on the inside of his eyelids. His ears rang with the dead man's unearthly screams. He'd done it, the unthinkable. He'd distilled another human being. The deepest, darkest level of Hell was reserved for distillers... and he had just earned himself a seat at the Devil's table.

"Matt!" Radar called. "Wait up!"

Matt wrenched the door open, blinded by the sunlight. He ripped off his mask and gulped lungfuls of fresh air, not caring about the poisonous vapor it contained. A large man stepped into view and blocked out the light. "Hey!" he shouted.

Matt didn't think; he simply reacted. He snapped the Well Digger up and fired, unloading both barrels into the man's face at point-blank range. Blood and brain tissue splattered against the door and painted Matt's face and armor crimson. He blinked and stumbled back, caught off guard by the backsplash of gore. Through the roaring echo, he could hear shouting and multiple footfalls in the alley; his friend hadn't been alone.

Radar came to a skidding halt and slammed the door shut. He fumbled with the rusty lock until it finally clicked. Satisfied they were safe for the moment, he slumped back against the wall. His chest heaved, and his breath came in ragged gasps as he tried to catch it.

"You okay?" he asked.

Matt nodded as he fumbled with the knot of his bandana. He wiped his face with it, clearing as much of the blood away as possible. The door rattled as the men on the other side tried to break it down.

Matt thumbed the safety on the side of the Well Digger, deactivating the lower barrel to conserve ammo. He winced as a stabbing pain shot through his wrist. The Well Digger wasn't meant to have both barrels fired so carelessly. One had to steady the shot and prepare for the weapon's tremendous kick, or else risk injury.

Matt dropped the gun and rolled his hand in a circle. The bones in his wrist popped loudly, and he winced. The pain dissipated somewhat, and he collected the weapon.

He'd gotten lucky.

"What's going on?" Phoenix called out. She was helping Samuel out of the stairwell.

"The way's blocked," Radar answered.

Gunfire battered the door, raising buckshot dents on the metal surface like Braille.

"Go back!" Matt scrambled to his feet and pushed Radar toward the stairwell.

"What are you, nuts?" Radar staggered. "I'm not going back down there!"

Matt tried the door opposite the exit, but found it locked. He aimed the Well Digger at the lock. "Stand back!"

Flame spat from the Well Digger's top barrel, and the lock exploded into a mass of twisted, useless metal. Matt kicked open the door and raised his gun, but there was no sign of human life, only stacks of wood as high as his head. The chugging of heavy machinery grew louder.

Matt picked up Samuel and threw the old man over his shoulder. "Inside!" he ordered.

Phoenix went first, followed by Matt, with Radar covering their rear with his .38. The stacks of wood lined both sides of their path, some of it raw timber, but most of it miscellaneous scrap. Table legs, baseball bats, and nail-studded two-by-fours jutted out from the debris.

Behind them, Matt heard the outer door break open, followed by the footfalls of god-knew-how-many angry men. They would be on top of them at any moment, and there was nowhere to hide.

"Phoenix!" Radar called. "Help me!"

Matt turned. Radar was pulling logs out of the stacks and dumping them on the floor. Phoenix squeezed past Matt and joined Radar, removing logs from the middle of the opposite stack. As they worked, Matt saw one of their pursuers stick his head through the door.

He raised the Well Digger. "Get down!"

Phoenix and Radar ducked, but continued to work, pulling at the lower logs. The pirate saw Matt and closed the door to protect himself, but Matt fired anyway. The bullet tore through the rusted metal and then did the same thing to the man's chest.

"Holy fuck!" a voice from behind the door shouted.

"Forget it," Matt yelled. "Let's go!"

"Almost got it!" Phoenix grunted as she tugged on a stubborn log. Finally the wood pulled free, and the stack leaned precariously. Phoenix grabbed Radar by the wrist and yanked him out of the way before the entire stack tumbled down, blocking the path with a chest-high pile of debris.

"That should buy us some time," said Phoenix.

"Not enough," Radar huffed.

"Just keep moving," said Matt.

Sweat beaded on the weller's forehead, but not from exertion. The room was oppressively hot, and the air grew increasingly heavy and moist. Matt's clothes clung to his body, making him feel sticky and unclean. His boots slipped on the concrete floor, which was damp and covered with mildew.

When they came to a junction in the stacks, he could see the massive steam engines to his right, their pistons pumping and chugging. White vapor spewed from breaks in the pipes that carried the steam to the rough holes in the ceiling. Workers wearing heavy gas masks split logs and broke lumber, then tossed the wood into roaring furnaces to fuel the machines; they were too absorbed in their work to notice the intruders.

The large loading bay door they had seen from the street stood to their left, but it was closed now. Radar ran to it and tried to lift it, but couldn't budge it more than an inch. It was locked from the outside. They could tear it off the track, but it would take time.

Time was something they were fresh out of.

Matt wiped moisture from his forehead with the back of his gun hand and walked toward the steam generators. He thrust the Well Digger into the face of one of the wood splitters. "Hey!"

The startled man raised his axe defensively.

"Drop it!"

The worker, his eyes fixed on the gun, nodded and complied. His partner did the same.

Matt blinked, sweat stinging his eyes. "Where's the way out?"

The man cocked his head to the side, directing his ear toward the weller.

"The. Way. Out," Matt shouted. "Where is it?"

The workers pointed over Matt's shoulder, toward the lumber stacks.

Matt shook his head. "Where's the back door?"

The workers looked confused.

Light poured into the building from behind the weller.

"There they are!"

"Shoot 'em!"

A bullet whizzed past Matt's head and struck one of the wood splitters in the neck. The man clutched at his throat and sank to his knees.

Matt whirled and fired at one of the silhouettes framed in the open doorway. Blood splashed from the man's shoulder, and he dropped his gun. As he knelt to retrieve the fallen weapon, Phoenix shot him in the head, sending the man's body spinning to the ground. The others retreated behind the edges of the door.

"Fall back!" Radar shouted as he popped off a quick shot at a pirate brave enough to peek inside.

Matt led them behind the chugging steam engines. The sound was deafening. A bullet ricocheted off a pipe near Matt's head; he had not even heard the report of the weapon that had fired it over the cacophony. He helped Samuel down to the ground and dug in his pack for fresh cartridges.

Samuel placed a frail hand on Matt's shoulder and, barely audible over the machinery, said, "You did your best, son."

Radar's .38 fired in rapid succession.

Matt slipped five new shells into the Well Digger's cylinder and snapped the breech shut. "We're not dead yet."

The old man's eyes were full of admiration, but the weller saw no hope there. Matt reached into his pack and produced a snub-nosed .22 revolver. He flipped the cylinder open, checked it, and flipped it shut again with a snap of his wrist, then handed it to Samuel.

"Eight shots," he said. "Make 'em count."

Samuel nodded and peered around the corner, then fired twice.

Radar sat beside Matt, his back to the steam engine, and dumped the spent, smoking shells from his .38. He rummaged in his pocket for fresh cartridges, coming up with only four. He cast Matt an exasperated look as he fed them into the cylinder.

"I need you to do me a favor, buddy," he said.

Matt didn't answer, but instead concentrated on reloading his own weapon.

"If I don't make it out of here," Radar continued, "bury me with a gallon of water, so I'll have something to bargain with when I get downstairs."

Matt laughed. "If I go, bury me with my gun."

"What the hell for?"

"When I meet the Devil, I'm gonna shoot him right between the eyes and take *his* water."

Radar grinned.

Matt snapped the Well Digger's breech shut and looked at Radar. "Race you to Hell."

Radar cocked back the hammer on his .38. "I'll give you a head start."

Matt grinned, stood behind a steam pipe for protection and took aim. The Well Digger roared over the engine. One by one, Koozy's men fell; they were easy targets framed in the doorway. A steady ringing grew in Matt's ears, the alternating chugging of the steam engines and the reports of numerous firearms fading away, muffled.

As if he was underwater.

He wiped his brow with his free hand. He *felt* like he was underwater. His clothes dripped and weighed him down. The contaminated steam made it hard to breathe. In his panic, he'd dropped his mask; not that he figured it would do much good so close to the source of Koozy's airborne plague.

If Koozy's men didn't kill them, the air probably would.

Bullets struck the steam outlet next to Samuel's head, and the pipe ruptured, spraying him with a jet of scalding vapor. Matt watched dumbstruck as the flesh melted off Samuel's face and blood ran freely to the ground. Samuel staggered out from behind the protective cover firing blindly at Koozy's men.

"Samuel!" Phoenix screamed; to Matt it sounded a thousand miles away.

Bullets from unseen automatic weapons tore through Samuel's body, and as he fell, his trigger finger continued to squeeze, even though his gun had already clicked empty.

"You bastards!" Radar shouted, or at least that's what it sounded like he said.

Radar fired his two remaining rounds, and then sank down to reload while Phoenix covered him with that pretty hand cannon of hers. Matt looked back at the open door and leveled the Well Digger at one of the blurry shapes standing in the center of the doorway. He squeezed the trigger. He fired a second and a third time before he noticed the absence of the familiar kick.

He felt something slam into his left shoulder, and his body bucked from the impact. He looked down and saw the hole in his coat, and the dark crimson stain spreading around it. It didn't hurt - at first - but when he tried to move, he felt an intense burning pain shoot down his entire arm. His fingers went numb, and he watched the Well Digger - empty and useless - fall to the wet floor.

"Matt!" he vaguely heard Radar shout.

Matt looked down at the blossoming bloodstain and clenched his jaw. He wrenched the machete from its sheath and stepped out from behind the engine, ready to charge the pirates if necessary, but before he could round the corner, he found himself staring down the barrel of a twelve-gauge pump-action shotgun. The pirate's lips moved soundlessly, the words lost in the ringing in Matt's ears, which was in turn being drowned out by his own heartbeat.

"Drop it, motherfucker!" the pirate shouted silently.

Matt looked over his shoulder and saw Radar and Phoenix on their knees, hands raised submissively. Radar looked up at Matt, the barrel of an AK-47 pressed against his head. It was over; it had been over before it even began.

Radar's lips shaped the unmistakable words, "I'm sorry."

Matt's fingers relaxed, and he let the machete clatter to the floor. He returned his gaze to his captor in time to see the butt of the shotgun coming toward his face. The world exploded in a flash of light, and then everything went black. The weller was unconscious before his body hit the ground.

# Twenty-Two

Matt was only dimly aware of somebody slapping his face, but the sensation slowly brought him back to consciousness. His mouth tasted metallic; it took him a moment to realize it was blood. He heard angry shouts, but the sound seemed so distant. He opened his eyes and immediately shut them against the impact of a gloved hand against his cheek.

"He's awake!" a male voice said.

"Help him up," said another. "He's bleeding on my carpet."

Matt opened his eyes as a bearded man grabbed him by his lapels and pulled him up onto his knees. The man stepped aside, allowing Matt to view his surroundings, but kept within striking distance. The room was large, and judging by the furnishings, an office.

A massive mahogany desk occupied the area between Matt and the window, which overlooked the city's pathetic skyline. A crystal pitcher filled with water caught the afternoon sun and cast a rainbow onto the threadbare carpet. Behind the desk, with his back to Matt, stood a man in a light brown suit.

This, Matt guessed, was the devil who answered to the name of Patrick Koozy.

"Mr. Freeborn," said Koozy. He paused to drink from the crystal tumbler in his hand. "I'm glad you could finally join us."

Matt unclenched his teeth to speak, and the pain in his shoulder flared. He took a deep breath and finally found his voice. "How do you know my name?"

Koozy turned. His face was handsome, clean-shaven and bespectacled. His skin was soft, lacking the leathery texture typical of wastelanders. His coal black hair was impeccably greased and parted on the right side. He grinned, showing a mouth full of pearly whites. Matt would have disliked him instantly even if he wasn't a ghoul. Koozy's right eye blinked and the corner of his mouth twitched, momentarily contorting his features.

"Your name?" Koozy said. "Simple. We asked your traveling companion."

Matt straightened up, despite the searing pain. "Radar?"

"Oh, don't be cross with him, Mr. Freeborn," Koozy said soothingly. "In fact, you should be proud of him. He didn't say a word until we took the second finger."

"What?"

Koozy pointed casually to his left. Matt looked and saw Radar huddled into a corner with a broad-shouldered pirate standing over him. His hand was clutched tight against his chest, wrapped in a filthy, crimson-stained towel. Slowly, shaking violently, he revealed his mutilated hand. Where the pinkie and ring fingers on his right hand should have been were two bloody stumps.

"I'm sorry, Mattie," he croaked.

Matt whirled on Koozy. "You son of a bitch!"

Matt prepared to lunge, but the pirate guarding him kicked his wounded shoulder and forced him back down to the floor. "Stay down!"

Matt slowly got back to his knees as Koozy sat on the edge of the desk.

Matt glared up at him. "I'll kill you."

Koozy chuckled as he filled his now-empty glass with ice from a small bucket beside him. "Sure you will."

Matt stared at the clear cubes clinking in the glass. Ice wasn't a simple luxury item. It was a status symbol. Desks and suits might not

142

have impressed him, but the ice told him everything he needed to know.

He'd shit in the wrong yard.

Koozy filled his glass from the pitcher, and Matt watched the ice swirl in the water, listened to it clatter and crack. Matt licked his cracked lips as Koozy raised the tumbler to his own and drank deeply.

"Ah!" Koozy held the glass out to his prisoner. "You look parched, Mr. Freeborn. Would you care for some?"

"I'd rather drink sand."

"I think we can accommodate you." Koozy's face twitched again.

Matt's brow furrowed as he watched Koozy's face. What *was* that? A side-effect of the air pollution, perhaps? With all of his creature comforts, Koozy didn't strike him as the type to wear a gas mask. Had the toxins in the steam caused permanent neurological damage?

Koozy took another drink. "You two have caused me a lot of trouble. Killed my men, wrecked their vehicles, destroyed my distillation machine, and killed its operator. And for what? A *truck*?"

Matt looked into Koozy's eyes. "My friend's very fond of his truck."

"Sentimental value," Radar rasped.

Matt couldn't help himself; he smirked.

Koozy scoffed. "Sentiment has little value out in the wastes."

"It's the little things that make life worth living," Matt said.

Koozy pointed at Matt with the hand holding the glass. "At last we agree on something."

Matt looked around the room. "Where's Phoenix?"

"Mayor Phoenix has been stripped of her office." Koozy stood and walked back to the window. "She will serve as an example to the people of her town. Rebellion will not be tolerated and shall be dealt with harshly."

"How?"

"How else?" Koozy glanced over his shoulder at Matt. "She'll be hanged for her crimes."

Radar tried to jump to his feet, but was quickly thrown back down. Koozy smiled, and his face twitched again.

"And what about us?"

"Well, that presents an interesting problem," Koozy said. "You are not residents of my territory, therefore your actions were not rebellious. However, reparations *must* be made. You are men of the wastes. It's only fitting that I return you to the wastes."

Matt looked at Radar, who wore an expression of confusion similar to his own, then back to Koozy. "I don't understand."

"Ah, here they are now." Koozy beckoned to Matt.

The pirate pulled Matt up by the collar and herded him behind the desk. Matt stood beside Koozy and stared at him for a moment before following his gaze to the street below. His eyes grew wide and he slapped his palm against the glass. Six stories down, a wrecker driven by Koozy's men came to a stop in front of the building. Behind the truck... was the Road Runner.

Matt lunged at Koozy, intent on throttling the man with his one good hand, but the pirate caught him across the throat with his forearm and sent him sprawling to the floor. Matt coughed, tears welling in his eyes. When he finally caught his breath, Koozy was standing over him with the Well Digger.

"It's really quite simple, Mr. Freeborn," Koozy said. "You have robbed me of my livelihood, so I must respond in kind. I will send you back out into the world the same way you entered it - naked."

Matt seethed. "You're going to wish you'd killed me."

"I have." Koozy's face twitched. "Bag them."

Before Matt could react, a heavy canvas sack was thrown over his head, and the world went dark again.

# Twenty-Three

"Where are you taking us?" Radar demanded, his voice quavering.

They'd been driving for thirty minutes. In what direction, Matt couldn't be sure. Koozy's men weren't talking. Radar was lying beside him in the bed of the pickup - *his* pickup. Radar had recognized the sound of the engine immediately.

It only added insult to injury.

The wellers were naked, save for the canvas bags tied over their heads. Their hands were bound behind their backs, which wasn't doing Matt's shoulder any good. Through the sacks, he could hear Radar's labored breathing. He had no idea how much blood his friend had lost, but he was certain that if they didn't get him some help soon he'd be dead by sundown.

"Scott," he whispered. "How you doing?"

Radar took a deep, rattling breath. "Not too good if you're using my real name."

Matt swallowed, a painful action considering how dry his throat was. The wind whipping at his body slowly calmed as the truck came to a stop, the tires skidding on loose sand and gravel.

"What's going on?" Radar asked.

"We've stopped," Matt said.

"I'm losing blood, not brains," Radar snapped. "Where are we?"

Matt listened as the pirates exited the truck, walked to the back, and lowered the tailgate. Gloved hands grabbed onto his ankles and he was pulled from the bed. His heart jumped into his throat as he felt himself falling. The impact with the hot asphalt knocked the air out of his lungs and jarred his wounded shoulder. A moment later, he heard Radar land beside him.

"Welcome to Cedar Rapids, boys!" one of the pirates laughed. The others joined in, hooting like a pack of coyotes.

"Cedar Rapids!" Radar shouted.

"Ye'siree!" a pirate jeered. "City of Five Seasons."

"Let's see," said another. "That's fall, winter, spring, summer, and uh... What's that last one again?"

"Fallout!"

The pirates erupted into a renewed fit of laughter. One by one, Matt heard them pile back into the truck. The engine roared, and it took off, spinning its tires and spraying the wellers with rocks and sand as it whipped around. As it passed, one of the pirates shouted, "Enjoy your stay, boys!"

Matt and Radar listened as the truck roared off into the distance. When the sound had faded, Matt realized Radar was crying.

"Scott? Radar!"

"We're going to die!" Radar sobbed.

"Stow that shit!" Matt grunted as he struggled up onto his knees. "Get it together."

"What's the point?" Radar whimpered. "We're blind. No food. No water. No chance in Hell. The radiation will cook us alive if we don't bleed to death first."

"I ain't dead yet." Matt nudged Radar with his knee. "Now get up."

"Leave me."

"Goddammit, Scott, you dust-for-brains!" Matt kneed him again in the ribs. "We're not dead yet. Now get your carcass up, and don't make me tell ya again!"

Matt listened as Radar slowly got up onto his knees, and finally rose to his feet with a grunt. Matt followed, making sure to keep his body against Radar's to keep them from becoming separated.

"Watch it!" Radar exclaimed.

"What?"

"That's my dick you're rubbing up against."

"Is that what that was? I thought I found your little finger."

Despite the pain, Radar laughed. Matt was relieved to hear it. It meant they hadn't broken him completely. Or was that delirium setting in?

"Now what?"

"They went that way." Matt nudged Radar's shoulder with his own, wishing he hadn't. The pain was excruciating. "I say we follow."

"And go right back to Koozy?"

"You have a better plan?"

"I already told you my plan. You voted me down."

"Then we walk. Come on. Stay with me."

"Lead the way."

They walked, attached at the shoulder, heading in what direction they hoped was south. As the blistering sun bore down on his naked skin, Matt hoped that was the only thing slowly cooking him.

*****

"Marco!" Radar shouted. They'd drifted apart again.

Matt took a step to the right and felt Radar's hot, sweaty shoulder against his own. "Polo," he replied.

They took a few stumbling steps in silence before Radar found his voice again. "Think we're... out of the... hot zone yet?" His voice was getting weaker.

Matt shook his head. "I dunno. No telling how far in they dropped us off."

He'd tried to count their steps, but between his own exhaustion and trying to keep Radar talking, he'd soon lost count. When he bruised his knee on the bumper of an abandoned car, he stopped caring. The light bleeding through his bag was fading, however, and the air was beginning to cool. Night would soon be upon them.

Another few steps and Radar gasped, "I think I need to sit down."

"Keep moving," Matt said. "We have to keep walking."

"I..." Radar staggered. "Can't."

Matt felt the cool wind against his shoulder and heard Radar's body fall to the ground. "Radar! Radar, get up!"

Silence.

Matt felt along the ground with his foot until he touched Radar's leg. He called out again, but still received no answer.

"Radar!" he shouted. "Help! Somebody help us!"

He fought desperately against his bonds as he shouted, but it was no use. The pirates had tied them too tight, and his struggling was only making the cord cut deeper into his wrists. The wound in his shoulder burned as he fought, but it only fueled his rage and frustration.

*"Somebody!"*

Exhausted, he collapsed to the ground beside his friend. He bellowed as a piece of gravel dug into his ass, and he fell onto his side.

"I'm sorry, Radar," he whispered.

Matt became still and held his breath, listening for Radar's. It was thready, but it was there. Another sound, growing louder by the second, caught his ear. He lifted his head off the pavement to listen, half afraid and half jubilant. It was mechanical...

An *engine!*

"Help!" he struggled up onto his knees. "Help us!"

Light bled through the fabric, and Matt began to thrash, trying to move enough to attract attention. The engine grew louder until it became a roar, and the light pouring through the fabric blinded him. Brakes squealed, and the vehicle came to a stop a few feet from the wellers. Matt listened, his body tense as the door opened and someone got out. Heavy boots thumped on asphalt.

"Please." Matt looked up at the shapeless figure blocking out the light. "Help us."

A knife clicked open, and Matt recoiled. Rough hands caught him behind the neck and held him up.

"Calm down, young fella," a gravelly voice said.

Matt felt the hands tug on the cord around his neck. The blade sliced through, and the tension slackened. The bag was pulled off his head, and Matt found himself looking into a bearded, wrinkled face. On any other day he would have declared it the ugliest mug on a non-mutant, but at that moment the old codger's face was tied with Phoenix's ass for first place in the "Things Matt Freeborn wants to clamp his lips onto" contest.

"You hurt bad, son?" the old man asked as he cut the cord around Matt's wrists.

Matt's shoulder felt both better and worse as he moved his arms for the first time in several hours. "Shot. But my friend—"

"I'll take care of him." The man pulled Matt to his feet and led him to the vehicle, which Matt realized was a tan military Jeep. "You just lie back."

Matt sunk into the passenger seat, still mumbling as the old man, illuminated by the headlights, scooped Radar's limp body up into his arms. With Radar safe, Matt allowed himself to succumb to exhaustion and injury. He was asleep before the Jeep rumbled off into the wastes.

# Twenty-Four

A sharp chemical smell stung Matt's nostrils, and he awoke with a start, swatting at his face. When his vision cleared, he saw the old man crouched in front of him with a brown plastic bottle in his hand. He offered the bottle to Matt and said, "Drink."

Matt took a tentative sip and gagged.

*Iodide!*

Matt almost spat the offending liquid at the old man's face, but then he remembered where he'd been and realized why he was making him drink. He was being treated for radiation sickness!

Matt snatched the bottle from the old man's hand and took a long hard pull. He coughed and gagged as the foul liquid churned in his stomach.

"That's enough, son." The old man patted him on the back lightly. Matt belched. "Won't do you any good if you puke it all up."

Matt leaned forward and put his head between his knees, sucking in great lungfuls of cool air. Finally the nausea dissipated somewhat, and he sat up. He was seated in a high-backed chair in the middle of a large room lined with bookcases. He scanned the titles on the spines; instead of literature as he would have expected, they were manuals for vehicles and machines of all makes and models. A fire crackled in a brick fireplace along one wall.

"Can you stand?"

Matt nodded.

"Good. Help me out with your friend."

Matt slowly got to his feet, ignoring the searing pain in his knees, and followed the old man to a blue couch where Radar lay limp and silent. Matt knelt beside the couch and placed his hand on Radar's chest, relieved by the steady heartbeat. His skin was pale and clammy, a bad sign.

"Try to rouse him," the old man said.

"Radar." Matt placed his good arm behind his friend's back and lifted him gently. "C'mon, dust brain, wake up."

Radar's eyes fluttered and rolled for a few moments before finally focusing on Matt. "Don't... call me dust brain... dick licker," he mumbled.

Matt let out a coughing laugh. "C'mon, buddy. I need you to drink. It's going to taste like shit, but you need to drink it. You hear me?"

Radar nodded weakly.

"Okay. Here it comes." Matt moved aside to let the old man raise the iodide to Radar's lips. "Down the hatch."

For a moment, it seemed as if Radar would drink the disgusting fluid peacefully, but then the taste hit him and he began to thrash. The old man managed to get some of the iodide into him before he wretched. Matt clamped his hand down over Radar's mouth to keep him from vomiting.

"Swallow it!" Matt winced as Radar fought to pry his wounded arm away. "Swallow!"

Left with no other choice, Radar swallowed the mouthful of iodide and bile, and then relaxed against Matt's arm. His eyes, now alert and angry, we're locked on Matt's. *You rotten son-of-a-bitch*, they seemed to say.

"Come on now, son." The old man brought the bottle back up to Radar's lips. "Drink."

Radar reluctantly took the bottle. Tears welled from his eyes as he drank. He sputtered and coughed as the last drops trickled down his throat.

"Radar, huh?" The old man screwed the cap back on the bottle and looked at Matt. "I suppose that makes you Hawkeye."

Matt stared at the old man. "What?"

"Nevermind." The stranger offered Matt his left hand. "Name's Axl."

"Matt." The weller winced as he shook Axl's hand.

Axl's eyes fell on Matt's shoulder. "We'd better get you boys patched up."

"Radar first."

Axl nodded. "Follow me."

*****

Matt screamed and bit down on the stick in his mouth so hard he thought his teeth might break. He was lying on a kitchen table while Axl stood over him and probed the hole in his shoulder with a pair of needle-nosed pliers. They were still hot from the boiling water he'd sterilized them in.

Radar sat in a chair against the wall, wrapped in a blanket and sipping broth from a Daffy Duck coffee mug. His right hand was heavily bandaged, and he was beginning to regain some of his original color. He'd almost thrown up the iodide again when Axl showed him his hand, but by some miracle he managed to keep it all down. Koozy's men had used side cutters to remove the digits, and had made quite a mess of the surrounding tissue in the process, but Axl did the best he could to mend it.

Matt heard a loud crunch, and Axl twisted the pliers. He screamed, and the stick fell from his jaws.

"There we are." Axl pulled gently. "Almost there."

Matt gritted his teeth and panted as Axl wiggled the pliers up and out of the wound. Finally the tool pulled free of the bloody opening, and Matt gasped. Axl held them up to the oil lamp hanging from the ceiling to examine the bullet.

"Ah, nine millimeter." He dropped it into a ceramic bowl on the table.

Matt relaxed and closed his eyes. In all his years welling, he'd been shot four times - once with an arrow - but they'd all been grazes. He'd never had to dig a slug out before, and he hoped he'd never have to experience it again. Axl gave him a white cloth and instructed him to hold it tight over the wound; Matt complied.

Axl produced a needle and thread. "So what did you boys do to get yourselves dropped off in the middle of the hot zone wearing naught but your skin and a couple of feed sacks?"

Matt removed the cloth to allow Axl access to the wound. "You ever hear of Patrick Koozy?"

"We've met." Axl pierced Matt's skin with the needle. "Don't look at it, son. Look at me."

Matt inhaled sharply through his teeth and picked a pockmark on the old man's forehead to stare at. The sensation of the heavy thread being dragged through his skin gave him the chills.

"Exile's not Patrick's style." Axl tugged the thread taut and continued working. "He'd sooner kill ya and drink ya. How'd you two earn such special treatment?"

"We broke his extractor." Radar said.

Axl abruptly stopped suturing and looked into Matt's eyes. "You destroyed the machine?"

Matt nodded.

A smile spread over Axl's face. "Good lads."

Matt smirked.

"Wish I'd done it myself," Axl muttered. "When I had the chance."

"So you've seen it?" Matt asked, happy to keep the conversation going so long as it took his mind off his shoulder.

"Of course I have." Axl paused to tie off the last stitch and cut the thread. "I built it."

"You *what?*" Matt bolted upright, knocking Axl's tools to the floor.

"Now calm down or you'll bust your damn stitches." Axl pushed Matt down onto the table. "It was a different time. Things were a lot more chaotic in those days."

"That help you sleep at night?" asked Radar.

"No." Axl sighed. He turned to address Radar. "You boys wellers?"

Stony stares from both men answered him.

"Yeah, I had a feeling." Axl pressed a fresh bandage against Matt's shoulder and began wrapping it. "The Well Diggers' Union put a whole lot of effort into demonizing distillation in the early days. Told people we were vampires that snatched babies from cribs, that we were grave robbers... Hell, I don't have to tell you boys. You've had it spoon fed to you from the moment you were born."

"Don't try to sell us on it, old man," Radar snapped. "We've seen it, remember?"

"Why'd you build it?" Matt asked.

Axl sighed and finished Matt's dressing, then brought him a cup of broth. Radar begrudgingly allowed him to top off his own. Axl leaned against the kitchen counter.

"Like I said," Axl began, "it was a different time. I was an engineer in the Army when the bombs fell. We tried our best to restore order and infrastructure, but after word spread that Washington was gone and the government had fallen apart, well, most of us just didn't see the point anymore. No sense in just waiting for the Chinese to roll on in and finish us off. My unit disbanded. A lot of men became bandits, using their training to survive the only way they knew how. Some - like me - joined the migration to Mexico. *That* was where I met Joseph Koozy, Patrick's father.

"After the three-year winter, Joseph took it upon himself to rebuild society. He decided to start in Iowa City. It sits on a major crossroads, which made it a logical transportation hub. Being a Hawkeye, Joseph wanted to reopen the university for a whole new generation of thinkers, to preserve the arts, law, medicine, engineering. Joseph saw the war as a hiccup, a minor setback for mankind, even an opportunity. A chance to get back to basics. In a way, I suppose he was right.

"When we got to Iowa City, we found the suburbs occupied - refugees from Cedar Rapids, mostly. As you can imagine, water was a problem. The Iowa River was clean enough for our needs, but we knew rerouting the city's water supply would take time. So to ease some of the burden, Joseph and I decided to take a page from the bigger cities' book... Distilling.

"We converted the dead - *just* the dead, and for the most part everyone was happy. We used steam power to light a few districts of the city, and we even finished the Iowa River pipeline, but then..."

"What?" Matt asked.

"There was a drought," Axl continued. "We couldn't supply water for the people *and* power the city at the same time. There just wasn't enough to go around. When we shut off the power to conserve water, the people rioted. Joseph was forced to hire gangs as peacekeepers. That went over like a lead balloon."

"So you piped in contaminated water from the north to power the steam generators," said Radar.

Axl nodded. "We had no idea just how bad the water was when we began piping it in. After a while, people started getting sick, but we never imagined it was the generators causing it. By the time we realized what was wrong, it was too late."

"What happened?" Matt asked.

"Joseph died." Axl looked down at the floor. "Cancer, I reckon."

"And Patrick took control of everything his father had built."

Axl nodded. "Distilled his father before his blood was even cold and threw the body into the street for the dogs to gnaw on. He shut off the power to the residential districts, and there were riots in the streets. He restored order by having all dissenters distilled alive. There were so many rebels that he was able to stop drinking from the river altogether. He developed a taste for it, you see, the dead water, so now he uses the culling to keep his glass filled."

Matt could picture the swirling ice cubes in his mind, clinking in the glass. The thought made his teeth grind.

Axl sighed. "Patrick's father built an oasis, a desert paradise. That spoiled child turned it into a slaughterhouse."

"You're a soldier," said Radar. "Why didn't you do something?"

Axl scoffed, "Me? I'm an engineer. Just because the Army put a gun in my hands doesn't make me a warrior. Besides, what can one man do against Patrick's army of thugs?"

Matt nodded. "You're right."

Axl nodded, acceptance and defeat in his eyes.

Matt stood. "Two men would stand a much better chance."

Axl's jaw dropped, shocked by what he was proposing.

"Hell yeah!" Radar exclaimed.

"Not *you*, dust brain," Matt snapped. "Look at you. You're walking death. You wouldn't last five minutes."

"Screw you, turd driller!" Radar limped over to his friend and threw his coffee mug on the floor, not taking his eyes off Matt as it shattered. "Look at my *fuckin' hand*! I owe Koozy a much harder ass kickin' than *you* do. So if you think you're going to make me sit this one out, you've got another thing comin'!"

The wellers locked eyes, Radar staring down his shorter, unblinking friend. For a moment, it looked like they were going to throw down right then and there, but finally Matt slapped Radar on the shoulder.

"Fine," Matt conceded. "Your funeral."

"Not mine," Radar corrected him.

Matt smirked.

"Wait a minute." Axl stepped between them. "Are you boys really serious about this? Because if you are then we need time to plan—"

"No time," said Radar. "No plan."

"Koozy's going to execute Mayor Phoenix," Matt explained.

"No," Axl gasped. "That sweet girl."

"It's our fault Koozy has her," said Matt. "Will you help us?"

Axl didn't hesitate. He nodded. "What do you need from me?"

"Guns," said Matt. "Big fucking guns."

"And some wheels," Radar added. "Big, skull-crushing wheels."

"Come with me." Axl beckoned to the wellers and left the room.

"Hey, Axl," Radar called as Matt helped him to his feet. "You got some clothes we can borrow? Axl?"

*****

The wellers stood outside of a large metal storage building while Axl fumbled with a ring of keys.

"Light!" Axl barked.

Matt held the lantern higher, until the light glinted off the keys in Axl's hands. The old man grunted and resumed flipping through them, muttering to himself.

The wellers fidgeted with their new clothes, which were ill-fitting and smelled overpoweringly like Axl. Matt wore baggy black pants that were cinched around his waist with twine, boots that were at least two sizes too large and stuffed with magazine pages to make them fit, and a moth-eaten brown serape. Radar's pants rode so high that nearly a foot of skin showed between the cuffs and his duct-taped shoes. A faded Iowa Hawkeyes football shirt barely covered his long torso.

Matt swung the lantern toward Radar, who was shaking slightly. "How you holdin' up, Radar?"

Radar leaned against the roll-up door. "I'll be okay."

"You sure?"

Radar nodded.

"Light!"

Matt rolled his eyes and returned the lantern to Axl.

"Here we are!" Axl slipped a gold key into a padlock at the bottom.

Matt handed the lantern to Radar and helped Axl lift the overhead door, which got hung up on its track and had to be forced the rest of the way. Matt squinted into the gloom and held out his hand for the lantern. As he followed Axl into the building, the light chased the shadows away, and a large shape came into view.

Matt's jaw dropped.

"Axl?" Radar took a limping step closer. "Is that what I *think* it is?"

Axl grinned. "Beautiful, isn't she?"

"Where did you get it?" Matt asked.

"Ol' Joe and I cleaned out the National Guard armory after the first electricity riots," Axl explained. "Had to make a few modifications over the years. She sucks fuel like you wouldn't believe. When Patrick took control, I decided it was time for me to leave. I, uh - *liberated* this and a few other odds and ends."

Radar peeled his eyes away to look at Axl. "And Koozy just let you *take* it?"

"Just who was going to *stop* me?" Axl snorted. "What do you boys think? She big enough for you?"

Matt grinned. "She'll do."

# Twenty-Five

Patrick Koozy squinted and shielded his eyes from the early morning sun. He looked out over the crowd, a ragged and pathetic lot. They'd crawled out of their slums to show their support for their mayor, but had quickly calmed down after his men fired a few warning shots overhead. He wrinkled his nose; the smell coming from the crowd was repulsive, a lot like his men but in a more concentrated dose.

"How much longer?" he asked the man to his right.

The pirate had finished tying a hangman's noose and swung the rope a few times before letting it sail over the streetlight. He gave Koozy a thumbs up.

Koozy's face twitched. "Let's get this over with, then."

The hangman whistled and two pirates exited Koozy's building with Phoenix between them, her hands bound behind her back. She struggled and bucked against her captors, managing to knee one of the men in the groin. The crowd cheered as the man collapsed, clutching his bruised testicles. This earned Phoenix a backhand across the face from the other pirate that knocked her back a few steps, but she kept her footing.

Koozy's face twitched again. "Quit screwing around and bring the bitch here!"

The pirates obeyed, the one hunched and limping. When she arrived at Koozy's side, he looked her up and down. He eyed her bare feet and smirked. Her clothes were ripped and hung so loose he wondered if they were always like that or if his men had relieved her of more than her boots during the night.

Koozy's eyes travelled up her body to her face, to those fiery eyes. "Last chance to beg for mercy."

"So beg," Phoenix said.

Koozy chuckled. "Goodbye, Madam Mayor."

Phoenix made a wild swipe at Koozy with her legs as the pirates stood her on a wooden box. She flailed and kicked, but became still as the hangman cinched the noose around her neck. He checked the slack on the rope and nodded to Koozy.

Koozy turned to face the crowd. "Good morning." His face twitched.

Jeers from the crowd answered him. He ignored them and continued speaking.

"Rebellion," Koozy said. "Bloodshed in the streets. I thought we'd seen the end of this, but obviously some of you - like Mayor Phoenix here - need a reminder of the penalty for rebellion in *my* city."

"*This* isn't the city your father built!" an old man in the crowd yelled. "*This* is a prison!"

The crowd erupted into shouts of agreement.

The pirates leveled their weapons at the crowd, and the shouts subsided.

"My father." Koozy's face twitched twice. "What my father built was a marvel of post-war society. If not for my father, you would all be stumbling in the dark, sowing dead soil, and begging for water from bottom feeders like those outlanders you sent to kill me. Is *this* how you show your thanks to my family?"

"You're *nothing* like your father," said Phoenix.

Koozy looked up at the condemned woman, "You're right. My father didn't have the strength to do what was necessary to protect his investment. Luckily I do. Phoenix Dunn, you are guilty of treason against Iowa City and its steward. For your crimes, you have been sentenced to death. Do you have anything to say?"

"Yeah." Phoenix spat on Koozy's face. "Fuck you!"

Thunder rumbled in the distance.

Koozy's face twitched. He removed his glasses and wiped them clean with a handkerchief, which he tossed to the ground in disgust. He turned to the hangman.

"Hang the cunt."

The crowd erupted into shouts of outrage and protest, but Koozy still heard thunder. He looked into the sky, but the clouds were white and fluffy. *Odd.*

A loud explosion startled Koozy and knocked him off balance. He staggered and grabbed onto one of his men for support. The sound echoed off the buildings, and the crowd of onlookers dropped to the ground. Another explosion rumbled through the streets, and Koozy saw smoke rising to the north.

"What is that?" the hangman shouted over the din of the crowd.

A third explosion, this one much closer, shook the ground, and Koozy's face twitched.

"The power plant!" he gasped.

Over the cries of the crowd, Koozy heard the sound he'd first mistaken for thunder growing louder. Above the constant rumble was another, more mechanical sound. It was rhythmic, like...

Like the chugging of a steam engine.

Koozy's jaw fell slack as a metal behemoth turned the corner, smoke belching from the smokestack rising from the back. Heavy treads chewed up the asphalt before coming to a creaking stop. On the side of the long cannon, Koozy could make out the words "WELL DIGGER II" crudely painted in white. The turret on top of the tank rotated until Koozy could see down the long barrel.

A hatch in the roof opened, and Radar Rice popped up into view, a tan army helmet sitting lopsided on his head.

"Hey, Koozy!" Radar flipped him the bird. "Got another finger for ya! How 'bout you come on over here and get it?"

"The wellers!" Koozy turned to his men. "Kill them! And kill that *bitch*!"

The pirates opened fire on the tank, and Radar quickly dropped back inside.

*****

Radar slammed the hatch. "That got their attention!"

161

Bullets pinged harmlessly off the tank's shell. Matt sat at the controls while Axl crouched in the back and shoveled coal into a roaring furnace.

Matt looked through the periscope. "I see Phoenix! Axl, gimme full steam!"

The engineer dropped his spade and twisted a valve on a nearby pipe. Steam whistled through the pipes, and the tank shuddered.

"Hold onto something," said Matt.

\*\*\*\*\*

Phoenix fell, and the noose tightened, choking off the scream in her throat. She kicked her legs, and managed to catch the executioner across the chin. The pirate staggered and fell onto Koozy. Phoenix's feet dangled mere inches above the ground. She pointed her toes, looking for any kind of purchase, but felt only empty air.

The rope twisted, and through the tears welling in her eyes, she saw the tank bearing down on her at breakneck speed. Koozy rolled out of the way in time to avoid being crushed under the treads, but the executioner wasn't so lucky. The tank rumbled past Phoenix's swinging body and crashed into the light pole, snapping it clean off at the base.

Phoenix was thrown to the ground along with the pole. The slack in the rope loosened the pressure somewhat, but it still dug deep into her neck and restricted her breathing. She rolled over and saw a pirate crouching behind a parked car across the street, aiming his gun at her.

The tank's turret rotated with a loud mechanical whir. Phoenix curled into the fetal position as the cannon fired and blew the car sky high, and the pirate along with it. She felt the heat flash against her skin for an instant before the fireball dissipated. Her lungs burned as she gasped for air.

She felt hands pawing at her neck and looked up to see Matt loosening the noose. Finally her airway cleared, and she sucked in a lungful of air. She rolled on the pavement, coughing and gulping air greedily while Matt freed her hands.

"Are you all right?" Matt asked.

"Do I—" She coughed. "Do I *look* all right? What the hell took you two so long?"

"I had to learn how to drive a tank."

"Oh, shut up!" she snapped. "Get Koozy!"

Matt stood, brandishing an M-16. "Yes, ma'am."

He scanned the street; his eyes stung from the thick, black smoke billowing around him. He saw no sign of Koozy.

"I see him!" Radar called from the open hatch. He was readying the mounted machine gun, intent on sawing Koozy in half.

Matt followed Radar's gaze and saw a flash of brown suit in the smoke. Koozy was making a break for it.

"I've got 'im!" Radar said.

"No!" Matt held up his hand. "You take care of Phoenix. Koozy's mine."

"*The hell* you s—"

Matt shot his friend a burning glare.

Radar held up his hands. "Hey, give him hell."

Matt nodded and walked into the smoke.

*****

Phoenix reached up and took Radar's hand, allowing the weller to help her onto the tank. She stood on the fender and turned to look down on the townspeople staring up at her.

"Listen to me," she shouted. "Patrick Koozy is not your master. And no matter what you might have heard, he is *not* a god. I'm tired of sleeping with one eye open, wondering when Koozy's men will come for me."

The crowd cheered in agreement.

"It's time we take back what's *ours*," Phoenix said. "Who's with me?"

The crowd roared and broke apart, chasing down Koozy's men and overpowering them, beating them with any pieces of flotsam they could scrounge from the street.

Phoenix smiled. She turned to look at Radar, and the smile faded from her face. His eyes had been fixed firmly on her backside.

"Sorry," Radar said. "I'm not one for speeches."

Phoenix rolled her eyes. "Move over."

She climbed down into the tank. The inside was sweltering, almost as bad as the power plant. A man worked in the back of the cabin, shoveling coal into a furnace. The man stopped working and turned. He wiped the soot from his face and grinned.

"Phoenix!"

Phoenix's jaw dropped. "Oh my God! Axl?"

She leapt at the old engineer, wrapping him up in a tight embrace. He rocked back and caught himself before he could fall into the furnace.

"I was afraid we wouldn't make it in time," he said.

"Hey, guys," said Radar from the hatch. "I don't mean to spoil the reunion, but we've got company."

Phoenix climbed up beside Radar and stuck her head into the cooler outside air. Several pirate vehicles barreled up the street toward the rioting townspeople.

Radar swiveled the machine gun. "Axl, get this beast rolling!"

Radar opened fire as the first pirate car rolled through the haze, shredding the hood and shattering the windshield. The tank lurched forward. Townspeople scrambled about the street like confused deer, unsure of where to go. Radar waved his arm at them, trying to usher them out of the way.

The tank struck the lead pirate car and slowly climbed the hood, crushed the windshield, and rolled onto the roof. The tank tilted forward, bringing the cannon eye level with the machine gunner atop the second car. The gunner shook. Radar grinned.

"Let 'em have it, Phoenix!" he yelled.

Radar dropped down into the tank as the cannon shelled the pirate car. He looked up through the hatch and saw the fireball erupt overhead. He glanced over at Phoenix and grinned.

Phoenix laughed. "I hope your friend's having as much fun as we are."

"Not likely," said Radar. "Axl! Full steam!"

# Twenty-Six

Koozy pressed the elevator's call button, but it was unresponsive to his touch. He jabbed it again, but it failed to light up.

The power! Those outlanders had cut the power!

He ran toward the stairwell. An explosion shook the building, and he tripped. He looked behind him and saw the redheaded weller stalking toward the building, an assault rifle in hand. Even across the distance, Koozy could see Death in his eyes. He scrambled to his feet and threw the stairwell door open.

Koozy was plunged into darkness as he slammed the door closed behind him. Gripping the handrail with a sweat-slick hand, he climbed the unseen stairs as fast as his legs could carry him. His frantic breathing echoed off the cold cinder block walls, mocking him like hushed laughter.

A misstep sent him crashing down. His shin struck the edge of a step, and pain surged through his leg. He reached down and felt blood oozing through a hole in his trousers. The lobby door opened below, and faint light illuminated the stairwell.

"Koozy!" Matt's voice boomed.

Koozy resumed his climb, trying to ignore the heavy footfalls below him. As he reached the next landing, he felt along the wall. His fingers brushed against a plastic plaque and the number "5" embossed upon it. One floor to go.

Gunfire erupted, and Koozy fell flat on the floor. He covered his head as bullets whizzed past and ricocheted off the steel railing. The cacophony gave way to reverberating echo.

"Marco!" Matt called.

Koozy gritted his teeth and took the last set of steps three at a time, ignoring the pain in his leg. When he reached the sixth floor door, he paused to listen. The weller was still at least two stories below him; it was hard to tell with the echo. He pulled the door open, making the futile effort to do so quietly, and slipped through.

*****

Hinges creaked. Matt looked up and saw a sliver of light illuminate the top of the stairwell. A shadow blocked it momentarily, and the door shrieked shut again. He was alone, but he could still smell Koozy's cologne. He pressed his back against the wall as he approached the door, expecting Koozy to be waiting for him, but when he opened it the hallway beyond was empty.

He stepped out of the stairwell. Worn carpeting padded his footsteps.

"Patrick Koozy," he sang softly. "Come out and play."

The door to a janitor's closet stood open, and a wheeled yellow mop bucket sat in the middle of the hall. Matt kicked it aside and thrust his rifle inside. Empty. Matt relaxed slightly.

Koozy leaped from the office across the hall, brandishing a mop. The wooden handle struck Matt's left shoulder with enough force to break the head off. Matt felt warm wetness seeping through his serape. His stitches had torn.

He swung the rifle around, but Koozy ducked under the line of fire. Bullets sprayed the wall. Koozy, now in possession of a crude lance, swept Matt's legs out from under him. Matt hit the ground hard and fumbled for the rifle, getting it up in time to stop Koozy from driving the mop handle into his chest. Koozy froze.

Matt smiled, relishing the look of horror on the bastard's twitching face. He squeezed the trigger, happy to blow Koozy to Hell, but the rifle clicked. Koozy grinned and raised the mop handle for the killing strike. Matt brought both knees up to his chest and kicked Koozy in the stomach, knocking him back into the opposite wall.

The men grappled for the mop handle, but Koozy was no match for Matt's strength. Matt wrenched the stick from Koozy's grip and slammed it into his face. Blood and teeth flew from Koozy's mouth as he fell to the floor.

Before Matt could bring the mop handle up, Koozy kicked his right knee. Matt bellowed as something popped and he collapsed. Koozy scrambled to his feet and ran through a door at the end of the hall.

Matt grasped his knee and howled in pain. Koozy may have just been a pretty face in a suit, but the bastard kicked like a mule. Gritting his teeth, Matt used the mop handle for support and slowly stood. He grasped the stick with both hands as he walked after Koozy, passing through a reception area complete with couches and ancient magazines. Sunlight poured through double doors at the other end of the room.

When Matt walked through the door, he found himself in Koozy's office, the same room where only mere hours ago Koozy had passed sentence upon him and his friend. Standing behind his desk, with the Well Digger leveled at Matt, was the ghoul himself.

Koozy's gun arm shook. "You... You... *Fuck!*"

Matt smirked. Even with the Well Digger, it was damn near impossible to look intimidating with blood dripping down your chin and two front teeth missing.

"It's over, Koozy," he said. "Listen."

As if on cue, the concussion from a tank blast struck the building. Koozy turned to look out the window, and Matt took a labored step forward. Koozy swung back around and thrust the Well Digger forward.

"Don't you fucking move!"

Matt ignored the warning and took another step. "You plan to shoot me with my own gun?"

Koozy tried to smirk, but his face twitched instead. "Rather poetic, I'd say."

Matt leaned on the stick. "Go ahead. It won't save you. You're finished."

"Shut up."

"Those people you've been shitting on your whole life are going to come up here and rip you a new asshole. Hell, I think I can hear them coming up the stairs right n—"

"I said shut the fuck up!" Koozy cocked back the hammer.

Matt craned his neck and scoffed. "If you're going to shoot me, at least take the goddamned safety off first, you dust-brain goat fucker. Jesus, you're embarrassing yourself."

Koozy's nostrils flared. His eyes flicked down to the switch on the side of the Well Digger. He flipped it with his thumb.

Matt sighed. "This is gonna hurt."

Koozy squeezed the trigger. "Goodbye, Mr. Freeborn."

Matt dove to the floor, and the Well Digger roared, both barrels firing simultaneously. The bones in Koozy's wrist snapped, and he dropped the gun. Koozy fell to his knees and screamed as he cradled his broken hand.

Matt got to his feet and hopped over Koozy's desk. He scooped up the Well Digger and checked the cylinder. Koozy had been kind enough to fully load it for him; four live rounds remained. He closed the breech and placed the smoking barrels against Koozy's head.

"Get up," he ordered.

Koozy clutched his wrist to his chest as he stood.

"Look at me, Patrick."

Koozy's trembling gaze met Matt's.

"You *might* be a god," Matt said. "Hell, who am I to say? But it takes a *man* to fire this weapon."

"Go to Hell," Koozy snarled through clenched teeth.

"I'll be along. Keep a seat warm for me."

Matt shoved Koozy in the chest, sending him crashing through the window. Koozy gripped the windowsill with his one good hand. He dangled, shouting obscenities while Matt carefully knelt in front of him.

"I almost forgot something, Patrick." He pressed the Well Digger's barrels against the knuckles of Koozy's ring and pinkie fingers.

"No!" Koozy shouted. "Please!"

"Radar sends his regards."

Matt unloaded both barrels, vaporizing Koozy's hand. Koozy was silent as he fell, perhaps too shocked to scream. He struck the ground flat on his back, but didn't die instantly. He stared up at the sky for a moment before gasping his final breath. His face twitched three times, and was still.

Matt watched Koozy for several moments. Satisfied that his enemy was dead, he fell back onto the floor, drew a deep breath and shouted a single word.

*"Ow!"*

# Twenty-Seven

*"Ow!"*

Axl cinched the cord around the splints on Matt's leg. "Don't be such a damn baby. There. Give that a test run."

Matt pushed off the Road Runner's fender and took a few slow steps, his right leg stiff as a board. It was awkward, but he could walk. He was back in his regular clothes, for which he was grateful, but Axl's serape was folded on the back seat. They were standing in Phoenix's driveway. Radar and Phoenix sat on the tailgate of Radar's pickup.

"Thanks, Axl," Matt said.

Axl nodded.

"You sure you don't want to stay?" asked Radar. "At least until your leg heals?"

"Yeah," Phoenix chimed in. "You don't have to leave yet. Stay with us. We could use you here."

"Days are getting colder," Matt said. "Best be moving on."

"Where will you go?"

"South, I think." Matt smiled. "Maybe work on my tan."

Radar scoffed.

Phoenix hopped down from the truck and stuck her hand out. "Thank you, Matt."

Matt took her hand and shook it. "My pleasure, Mayor."

He turned to Radar and started to stick out his hand, but instead wrapped him up in a tight hug. Matt patted his friend hard on the back. Radar, with his injured hand, returned the gesture more gingerly. They separated. Now came the really hard part, the thing they'd always had trouble doing since they were children.

"Take care of yourself, Radar."

Radar nodded. "Be seeing you, Freeborn."

Matt turned towards the Road Runner.

"Wait!" said Phoenix.

Matt and Radar turned to face her.

"Did you say 'Freeborn?'"

"Yeah," said Radar. "So?"

Phoenix crossed the driveway to the mailbox. She wiped away the thick layer of dust on the plastic, revealing faint painted letters underneath:

F R E E B O R N

*****

"I can't believe I didn't see it before," Matt said.

"How could you?" Radar observed. "Look at all that *hair!*"

Matt held the framed family photo in his hands. Smiling back at him, unmistakable now that he realized it, were his grandfather, grandmother, aunt, and...

"The boy." Radar pointed. "Is that—"

Matt nodded. The shit-eating grin was unmistakable. "My old man."

But Matt wasn't focused on his father. His eyes were glued on the man who'd really raised him. Gene Freeborn, no more than thirty in the photograph, had a full head of thick, red hair. His skin was fair, not yet ravaged by decades of sun and sand.

Phoenix reached into one of the desk drawers, pulled out a stack of loose, yellowed papers, and handed them to Matt. As he flipped through the pages, he saw sketches of muscular men in capes, buxom women, bizarre landscapes, and a familiar double-barreled revolver. In the lower left hand corner was a stylized signature: GF. Matt pulled the Well Digger from beneath his coat;

171

carved into the handle were the same letters, written in the same fashion.

Matt smiled and rubbed at his eyes.

"This house belongs to your family," said Phoenix. "It's yours."

Matt shook his head. "It's yours now. Thank you... For keeping these, I mean."

Phoenix smiled. "My pleasure."

*****

Matt adjusted the rearview mirror and took one last look before Iowa City disappeared over the horizon. He checked the road and settled back in his seat. *This* was home. He drew the Well Digger and placed it on the passenger seat next to the framed photograph of his grandfather's family.

As the Road Runner roared and wove between the abandoned cars, Matt felt at peace, perhaps for the first time since he struck out on his own. He reached into the glove box and rummaged through the collection of cassettes. He pulled out a case with a black label and pushed the tape into the deck. He nodded as the opening notes of Metallica's *Wherever I May Roam* filled the car.

Yes. This was home.

# Epilogue

The weller sidestepped the shriveled, partially-devoured carcass of a horse lying in the middle of the street and continued on his winding way through the carnage. He stopped a moment to examine the opossum carcass lying on the sidewalk before moving on. Nothing moved in the town but blowing sand and buzzards. One of the foul birds hopped in his path, and he gave it a taste of his steel-toed boot.

When he came to the inn, he found the door clawed and riddled with buckshot holes. He opened it slowly, keeping to the side in case the innkeeper was feeling trigger-happy. The sickly-sweet smell of vomit assailed his nostrils, and for a moment, he considered donning his bandana, but settled for leaving the door open instead. He approached the counter, which was cluttered with various gold watches, and rang the bell. A soft moan drifted up from behind. The weller craned his neck for a better look.

Sprawled on the floor - lying in his own vomit and excrement - was the innkeeper. A filthy makeshift bandage barely covered the festering bite wound on his right hand. He clutched a double-barreled shotgun in his left hand, but was obviously too weak to lift it. His bloodshot eyes grew wide in recognition as they focused on the weller, and another low, pleading moan escaped his toothless mouth as he reached his wounded hand out to him. The weller slammed a Mason jar full of crystal clear water on the counter, and the man's blistered tongue protruded feebly from between his cracked and bleeding lips.

"Let's get down to brass tacks, old man," said Matt. "How much for that whiskey in the back?"

Matt Freeborn will return in

# THE WELLER
## FEAR OF THE DARK

# About the Author

Adam J. Whitlatch has written dozens of short stories and poems spanning the genres of science fiction, fantasy, and horror. His published novels include *Birthright*, *The Weller*, and the official novelization to the animated film *War of the Worlds: Goliath*.

Adam lives on a small farm in southeastern Iowa with his wife and their three sons.

**www.adamjwhitlatch.com**

Made in the USA
Columbia, SC
15 March 2019